ABRACADABRA
MOONSHINE

Abracadabra Moonshine

And Other Stories

Stephen Halpert

S & T Publishing

S & T Publishing
P.O Box 323
Grafton, MA 01519
sandtpublishing.com

Printed in the United States of America

ISBN-13: 978-0615970493 (S & T Publishing)

ISBN-10: 0615970494

Abracadabra Moonshine is a work of fiction. Any similarity to persons living or dead is purely coincidental.

Abracadabra Moonshine is also available as an audio-book and e-book.

To reach Stephen Halpert and find information on forthcoming titles visit: sandtpublishing.com.

For Tasha

Introduction

It was just a few years ago Stephen Halpert began creating weekly short stories for a few lucky family and friends, as well as his weekly readers in *The Grafton News*. We would eagerly await each Sunday's episode to find out whether Magee the detective would persevere beyond his limitations as a dog to solve a murder mystery, or we'd enjoy the real-life adventures of Stephen and his wife Tasha negotiating domestic tranquility, and maybe we'd discover which magical appliance would this time awaken a family to their ancestors or their fates. Now some of these tales are gathered together in a cornucopia you can enjoy all at once!

Though Stephen is a professional writer, I had only ever known him as a wizard artist of collage, weaving together disparate bits of paper into magical worlds. It isn't surprising he can do the same with words. With each story over the years his universe grew and the collage formed, exploring the ties that bind people, ghosts, and turkeys together, the mysteries of flying shoes, or wallets that produce Confederate money, and pendants that grant wishes, until eventually all became one. *Abracadabra Moonshine and Other Stories* portrays a world filled with the dark and the light, the happy, the heartfelt, the insightful, and the sentimental, woven together with everything your imagination could ever want.

We are acquainted with Mr. Perkins, who is inflicted

with the ability to see everyone as the animal they are most like, and despite his awkwardness, finds himself loved. We discover what Barack Obama's office life is like. We follow Babe Ruth's time-travelling exploits which land him in Fenway Park. We even learn that government forces deal with monsters—it's knowledge you can apply! Of course let's not forget Blast the Wonder Pig who can teleport and is more sentient than originally imagined.

Although these are presumably works of fiction, Stephen has imbued in them 70 years of wisdom, spiced with wit and whimsy. And as he says of all his collages, "the pure joy and reward is in the making of them." My wish is that you enjoy reading them as much has he enjoyed painting them.

Alex Schmidt

Acknowledgements

Thanks to Tasha Halpert and Laura Lorenz for their devoted editorial assistance, to Charlotte Eckler for her editing and proofreading expertise, to James Hester for his design and preparation of this collection, and to Russ (Doc) Dingley for the cover layout.

Thanks to *The Grafton News* where "American Scene" first saw the light of day and many of these stories first appeared.

To Ken Slaughter, founder of funnywrite.com, who has featured many of these stories and whose encouragement has been invaluable.

And to my weekly readers in Grafton, Massachusetts and on-line around the world, whose comments continue to be greatly appreciated.

Cover Art: *Acolyte*, collage by Stephen Halpert
Author's Photo: Tasha Halpert

Contents

Grandma's Radio

Vera and her friends, Lydia and Mattie, were sitting around her kitchen table for their weekly afternoon tea. The three women chatted amiably in her cozy kitchen with its red plaid curtains and the old fashioned canisters on the counter. Vera's prized possession was her grandmother's small brown and yellow radio that she kept on the shelf over her kitchen counter. When her friends spoke of their jewels and other inherited treasures, Vera would point to her grandma's radio and simply say. "This is my treasure. It's magical. "Her friend Lydia smiled. "Of course it is. It was your grandmother's, right there..."

"No," Vera said. "There's more to it than that, a lot more."

"What then?" Lydia stirred more sugar into her tea. She determined that Vera was jealous of her jewelry.

"It's how it brings the past to life," Vera said. "Grandma and I used to listen to soap operas: *Our Gal Sunday*, *Helen Trent*, and *Stella Dallas*. Afterward, Grandma would close her eyes, put her hands over her radio and tell me what would happen next. When I asked her how she knew, she'd say that Helen, Stella or Sunday told her."

Lydia shook her head and frowned.

Mattie smiled. Her blue eyes sparkled. "You loved her very much. You miss her. Having her radio touches your heart, yes?"

"It's not the radio, exactly," Vera said.

"Then what is it?" Lydia snapped. She leaned back and patted her burnished curls. She was always changing her hairstyle. Her beauty parlor loved her.

Vera poured more tea. She smiled at her memories. "Grandma somehow could talk with them. When she closed her eyes and imagined them, they'd tell her things."

"The actresses you mean?" Mattie said.

"No," Vera said. "No, the characters themselves. She said when she'd do her imagining she'd see them sitting across from her at her table—just like I see the two of you."

"Spooky!" Lydia frowned, then, remembering she wanted to avoid frown lines, she stopped. "Sounds to me like she was delusional."

Vera leaned back in her chair and laughed. "She said maybe what was alive in the three characters appeared to her. She'd conjectured that, with maybe a million listeners every day, they had had real life breathed into them."

"Well, why not?" Mattie said with a smile. "As long as what she did made her happy, who cares whether it was real or not?"

"They were like sisters to her. She'd share her feelings with them," Vera sighed and shook her head. "She'd tell Sunday that Lord Henry was an egotistical fool who only brought her bad luck."

"She said that?" Mattie's eyes widened.

"And what's funny is that Sunday would reply that half the men alive were that way. But she loved Lord Henry and that made it all okay."

"Ridiculous!" Lydia shook her head. "How can people get hung up on such fantasies?"

Vera passed the coffee cake. "Helen Trent was always having trouble with men. She was the eternal victim, always thinking life could be different just around the corner."

Mattie nodded. "I've felt that way a lot."

"And Stella Dallas," Vera looked sad. "Her daughter taken from her. Continually getting the wrong message and being lied to."

Lydia straightened her skirt and brushed off a crumb. "Sounds like real life to me. No one ever said it was supposed to be easy."

Vera nodded and looked at the old brown and yellow Motorola. "I have no idea what life's supposed to be other than what it is."

"Really?" Mattie said. "And to try to understand why it is that way makes no sense. It just is."

Lydia's face reddened. "But if you understand why things are the way they are then you can do something about them, make changes. You know, grow."

"I guess," Vera said. "But it's still the way it is. Maybe we can make small changes, but don't you think our lives are predestined?"

"This conversation is beyond me," Lydia said, rising. "I need to go. I have a yoga class in a half hour. Thanks for the tea and that delicious coffee cake."

Vera smiled. "Stella Dallas gave me the recipe. She used to make it when she lived in Boston."

"Oh!" Mattie said. "That's why it's so good."

But Lydia held her ground. "You mean your

grandmother wrote down a recipe she heard on that show?"

Vera shook her head. "No, she never did that. Stella gave it to me herself."

Lydia's eyes widened. "I'm out of here." As she was leaving she smiled and waved. "See you all in the loony bin."

After she left Vera smiled and laughed. "I knew she wouldn't believe me but I decided to tell her anyway."

Mattie finished her tea. "I'm not going to ask you anything about that. Whatever you think is fine with me. People have a right to create their own little worlds."

She left soon thereafter. Vera tidied up the kitchen, washed the dishes and put away the coffee cake. Outside the streetlights were coming on. It seemed darkness came too early these days.

Shivering a bit, she put on her warm, woolen sweater. Then she got her radio down from the shelf. She put her hands over it and began to hum a tune she remembered from her girlhood. Slowly the shapes of three women materialized and sat down with her around the kitchen table.

The Blue Pendant

After they had sold their home and while they were waiting for the completion of their new condo, Jim and Donna put their possessions in storage and signed on for an around-the-world cruise.

Once they got back, they went to their storage to reacquaint themselves with their stuff.

Jim had been bored on the cruise and missed access to his library. He gazed happily at his collection, boxed and placed alongside the cardboard wardrobes, furniture and cartons of household items.

"We must be sure you have enough shelves for your books," Donna said. She looked around and wondered how they could have accumulated so much.

Jim peered into a box of books. "These aren't mine."

"They have to be," she said. "You have the only key to the padlock."

He took out several volumes. His eyes widened even more. "Believe me, these Mark Twain first editions are not mine. I wish that they were, but..." He peered at a pristine *Huckleberry Finn,* bound in its scarce blue cloth. He looked at Donna. "Worth thousands! I never had that kind of money to invest in rare books like this."

He set the volume down and continued to look through the box. Carefully, he turned the pages of a presentation copy of *Tom Sawyer,* inscribed by Twain himself. "An heirloom!"

Looking in another box, Donna held up the Belgium lace embroidered tablecloth. "This must be from my great aunt and I just forgot about it."

Jim ran his hand through what was left of his hair. "This *Walden* has notations by Ralph Waldo Emerson. Donna, Honey... this is crazy!"

She looked at him. "Maybe the moving company confused ours and someone else's storage. But no!" She shook her head. "We were here the whole time they were moving it in." She looked at an authentic Victorian doll house filled with furniture. "Was that from her too? I don't remember it, do you? I've always wanted one, but who could afford something like that?"

"I've always wanted the *Tom Sawyer*," he said. "I think I'd better call the moving company."

"And say what? That there's stuff in our storage we don't think is ours? They'd think we were crazy."

His hand shook as he touched Benjamin Franklin's copy of *Washington's Farewell Address*.

She smiled and took his hand. "Maybe if you saw it as good fortune and thanked the universe."

"Easy for you to say! Another example of your la-di-da ways."

"I beg your pardon!" Her eyes widened, her cheeks flushed. "That wasn't very nice of you. Talk about looking a gift horse—"

He cleared his throat. "Donna, things just don't appear out of the blue. There has to be a rational explanation."

She nodded. "I'm grateful for the doll house. Can't you be glad to have some old books you didn't even know belonged to you?"

He shook his head. "I can't even imagine what the insurance will cost."

"Why bother?"

"Because now my library's valuable."

"So what? It's not like ..."

He shook his head and shrugged. "I'm stumped. Let's go get lunch, come back and pick out the prints we want to take with us to the condo."

Donna was rummaging through a box of her sweaters. "In a minute. I really don't remember buying any of these imported cashmere sweaters." She looked at him. "Are you sure you didn't buy these to surprise me?"

He just stood there.

"Well if you did, I thank you. Lovely colors, especially the pink pullover."

He stroked one. "Bulky cashmere like this costs a fortune." He grinned. "Where'd you come up with the money?"

She put her hands on her hips. "First you call me a flake and now you accuse me of being foolish with money."

His face reddened. "I never accused you of anything. But how do you explain your good luck? Leprechauns?"

"Get your facts straight," she said. "They're Irish. The sweaters come from Scotland."

"Let's just go eat lunch."

Neither was especially hungry. They picked at salads, ordered slices of pie and then went back to the storage.

Jim pointed out the carton labeled "prints." Donna cut away the tape and opened it. They gasped. Instead

of the prints there were exquisitely framed original oils
signed by Monet, Van Gogh, and Renoir.

Jim's head was bursting. Tears filled his eyes. "All of
a sudden we've got the best of everything."

In a kind of daze, Donna said, "That's what I asked
for."

"What?"

"Remember on the cruise, when we stopped at Santa
Nicola? When we walked through the tourist market, an
old woman smiled at me. She held out a blue glass
pendant. As I paid her for it she told me to make a
wish."

"And..."

Donna shrugged. "I didn't know what to wish for, so
I just asked for us to have the best of everything."

He gulped. "Then it's all really ours?"

"I guess so," she said. "I'm sorry if it bothers you."

His eyes bulged. "And can you make more wishes?"

Her face fell. "I'm sorry, but I really don't think I
can."

"Why on earth not?"

"Don't you remember? When we got back I gave the
pendent to our granddaughter for her third birthday."
She smiled wistfully. "The blue in the glass so
beautifully matches the color of her eyes."

The Great God Pan

Marion Baldwin and Lydia Smythe were roommates and Psych majors at Clark University in Worcester. Tonight, on the eve of their 25th class reunion, both women, with Marion's husband, Brad, were having dinner in an artsy bistro near the campus.

"I was thrilled when you won the National Book Award," Marion said, brushing back a lock of streaked blond hair. "Your study of Jung, myth, and the supernatural was brilliant. And you haven't aged a day."

Lydia giggled. Her mane of auburn hair flowed over the shoulders of her white silk blouse. "It's been a lifelong quest."

Brad Baldwin smiled. "I don't put much stock in the supernatural." He wiped his handkerchief across his balding forehead.

Lydia shook her head. "Our lives evolve into what we dare to make of them. So many roads wind throughout us that, ultimately, we recognize our confusion and then manifest our destiny." She took a long sip of something that sparkled.

"You even sound like Jung," Marion said. Unlike Brad, Marion was in good shape. She looked as though she played tennis daily. "What are you writing now?"

Lydia lowered her voice. "Promise you won't laugh?"

"Never!" Marion said. "You're my hero! You can do no wrong."

Brad took a sip of his whiskey sour, took his cell phone from his pocket, and stared at it.

Lydia looked intently at Marion. "It's an exhaustive appreciation of the Great God Pan."

Brad looked up and chuckled. "You mean that goat-legged Greek god who plays pipes and gets drunk on wine?"

"You have him mixed up with Bacchus." Lydia smiled. "There's so much more to Pan." She lowered her voice. "Believe me. His spirit interpenetrates the entire Earth."

Their waitress served their entrées.

"Have you finished your research?" Marion wondered if Lydia had a significant other, but was too polite to ask.

"The library research part only," she shook her head. "Thank goodness I've finished searching out rare esoteric texts full of symbolic riddles." She sipped. "But I feel like I've hardly begun."

Marion leaned forward and touched her arm. "Begun what?"

Lydia peered about. Shadows played against the windowpanes. "I need to feel his essence more intimately." She thought she glimpsed a shaggy head. *How odd,* she thought.

Marion picked at her salad. "How?" She tilted her head and frowned.

"Encounters with Pagan priests and priestesses," Lydia said. "I've also been invited to ceremonies dedicated to Pan." She smiled to herself.

"You never did get married, did you?" Brad asked. He signaled the waitress for another whiskey sour.

"Not for lack of opportunity," Lydia said.

Marion frowned. "I can understand that; you're movie-star gorgeous. But why not?"

Lydia shook her head and sighed. "After love takes me for a spin, men I'd thought interesting begin to bore me." She frowned. "No! That's not exactly it. They're just not feral anymore."

She gazed at the darkened windowpane. Were those eyes looking in at her? She put her hand to her throat. Perhaps just a trick of the light, she thought.

Brad rolled his eyes. "What's that supposed to mean?" He pulled apart a sweet roll and slathered it with butter.

"Oh, dear," Marion said. "Have you gone and fallen in love with your Great God Pan?" She sighed. "Fall for a god and all other men pale by comparison!"

Lydia's eyes softened. "When I was little I had an invisible friend. We'd sit in my grandmother's garden and he always said he loved me until one day he disappeared."

She looked wistful and smoothed her auburn hair. She arched her back and straightened her shoulders. "The keys to accessing the supernatural are within us. We are the purveyors of our own mythology." She sounded as though she were lecturing. "Every myth, Joseph Campbell explained, directly paralleled aspects of our human behavior."

"What went on at those ceremonies?" Brad asked.

Lydia shook her head. "I could never reveal that; except to say that an inexplicable epiphany overcame me."

"Fascinating!" Marion beamed. "It's like you're living

your myth."

The waitress cleared their plates and served coffee.

Lydia smiled. "I hope my publisher realizes that when he reads my manuscript. He didn't seem too interested when I told him my research was about Pan. All he said was that mythology had fallen off lately."

Brad sat back and patted his rather large belly. "Good food! But especially in today's economy you can't expect a publisher to throw money at the irrelevant."

Lydia shrugged and looked at her watch.

"Don't pay any attention to him." Marion glared. "Brad hardly ever reads."

"I think we must go," Lydia said. "They're having that reception for our class."

They left the bistro and walked past a grove of trees on the edge of the campus. A shaggy figure burst from it and rushed toward them. Seizing Lydia, he threw her over his shoulder. Brad thrust out his hands. The figure turned and bared his teeth in a strange grin, then flung Brad to the ground.

Horrified, Marion stared at the horns protruding from his head. As she opened her mouth to shriek he clamped a gamy hand over it.

"Mine," whispered a low, guttural voice. He pushed Marion backwards onto Brad. As the figure turned and disappeared into the grove, Marion caught a glimpse of Lydia's face. On it was a look of sheer ecstasy.

Mr. Perkins' Shoes

On a snowy Saturday afternoon, Mr. Perkins was wandering through the mall when he saw Big Sole Discount Shoes. The orange and purple neon sign blinked hypnotically and he found himself drawn into the gigantic shoe warehouse. *What am I doing here?* he thought. *I've enough shoes: what I'm wearing, plus my best for church, and sneakers for the yard.*

Ever cautious and watchful, Mr. Perkins had to admit that the prices were extraordinarily low; genuine bargains. There was nothing like a bargain to push a slight smile against the edges of his lips and give him a good feeling of thrift.

Most of the men's shoes looked odd: wild multi colored slip-ons; sneakers that didn't require the usual shoelaces; imported Italian soft leather loafers with tassels; high-stepping boots advertised to keep one's feet warm and snuggly even in subarctic temperatures. Though sufficiently marked down, the prices still seemed a bit out of reach to him. Breathing a sigh of relief, he made his way toward the door.

The final clearance table caught his eye. Shoes originally priced at several hundreds of dollars or more were marked down to less than twenty dollars. Still that was a lot for a pair for shoes he felt he didn't need. Then his hand brushed up against the softest of leather, a pair of no-nonsense walking shoes like he had worn as a boy. There was only one pair, fortunately in his size.

They were priced at an astoundingly low seven dollars. *What a wonderful bargain*, he thought, *how can I possibly resist?* Sitting on a padded bench, he took off his everyday shoes and slipped on the new ones. They fit like a glove, the most comfortable shoes he had ever worn. What could possibly be wrong with them? Bargains like that don't just happen. There has to be a reason like a defective sole, a loose tongue, or even a heel that sways and wanders. Still slightly reluctant to buy them, he tried to take them off. They clung to his feet like lost souls. At checkout he pointed down at the new shoes. "I hope there's nothing wrong with these."

"You can return them within seven days," the bored kid at the counter said as he put his old shoes in a bag and handed it to him. Mr. Perkins feet moved him toward the exit. Before he knew it he was inside his car in the parking lot. He looked down at his new shoes and smiled. Obviously, in today's market leather like this had to be very costly. He turned on the ignition and started for home.

Usually from the mall he'd take a left, a right, and then a short drive down the highway to the right turn onto his street. This time he turned left twice, then right, and found himself in the parking lot of the ice cream shop. *What am I doing here?* he thought. Moments later he ordered a triple chocolate chip cherry pecan banana split.

Back home, he admired his new shoes. Oddly, at one glance they seemed a dark brown, at another, a deep cordovan, and then a polished high gloss black. Though he couldn't be sure of the color he did feel a strange fondness for them.

The next day when he walked into church Homer

Mertz, chair of the finance committee, immediately noticed his shoes. "Pretty upscale shoes you've got there." He laughed. "Don't tell me you won the lottery?"

"Really, oh thanks," Mr. Perkins felt flustered. No one had ever complimented his footwear before.

"Join the Mrs. and me for brunch afterwards," Homer said. "We're going to that new upscale joint over on Route 9."

"Well I suppose," he equivocated. "But isn't it a bit pricey?"

Homer laughed. "The man buys a pair of shoes like that and then kicks over a few measly bucks for lunch!"

"Well in that case…" Mr. Perkins said as the organist began playing the Prelude.

The service seemed to drag on indeterminably. On that particular Sunday the minister chose to cover every indiscretion cited in Deuteronomy, and it wasn't until shortly after noon that parishioners stumbled out to their cars.

"Ride with us," Mertz insisted. His wife looked at Mr. Perkins shoes and her eyes widened. "Quite something," she said softly.

By the time they reached the bistro every table was either taken or reserved. The maitre d' was insistent. There was no available seating.

"Poppycock," Mr. Perkins heard himself say. "That's ridiculous!" Usually quiet and mild mannered, he gasped as his right foot kicked out savagely at the maitre d' connecting directly with the man's left shin.

The man howled. Mrs. Mertz gasped and looked at Mr. Perkins with newfound admiration. She had wanted to kick that maitre d' herself but her manners had interceded.

"Restless leg syndrome," he stammered. "It comes over me when I'm hungry."

He felt his leg taking aim again but he quickly turned away.

"Out!" cried the maitre d'. "Out or we'll call the police."

"Maybe just burgers and fries," Homer Mertz said, guiding him toward the door. "Really, Perkins, I've never known you to be quite so forthright. Perhaps it's time you took a seat on the Finance Committee."

"They say that shoes make the man," Mrs. Mertz cooed.

Over the next week, Mr. Perkins and his new shoes were inseparable. By comparison, his two other pairs seemed shabby, almost disreputable. His everyday walkers had started to fall apart. Even though he had always cared for his dress blacks, they looked scuffed and smudged. He couldn't understand this, as he had only worn them to church.

Much to his surprise, Mrs. Mertz kept appearing at his door with offerings of homemade soup, peach cobbler or her prize blueberry pan dowdy. Each time she would sigh, gaze wistfully at his shoes, and then a dazed expression would invade her face.

At his first Finance Committee meeting he was handed endless columns of figures to check. "Church is a business, ya know!" Homer Mertz reminded the committee members.

"See here," Mr. Perkins pointed to one of the columns of figures. "There's an accounting error! Church has an extra five dollars in its coffers."

"Brilliant!" Homer Mertz proclaimed. "At the annual meeting you must be elevated to the Board."

"Yes!" Other finance committee members agreed and by the end of that evening Mr. Perkins was a very large cheese on a tiny platter.

"Big weekend shoe sale at Magic Feet," Homer Mertz said as they left. "The Mrs. suggested we go after church. Then grab a bite. We'll pick you up."

Again that Sunday the service ran late. This time the minister spoke of the unity between men and angels and how angels intercede in our lives. Mrs. Mertz was touched by the service. She kept clutching Mr. Perkins elbow as her shoes brushed against his.

"I adore your taste in footwear," she whispered as he climbed into their car.

Magic Feet was a new shoe outlet featuring discounted shoes from countries no one had ever heard of. They parked in the large lot and went in.

"Knotted rawhide," Mrs. Mertz said. "Would my feet look good in rawhide sandals?"

"Look at those, Perkins," Mr. Mertz proclaimed. "Patent leather slippers. The kind any boy from a good family wore as a kid. Why not splurge and spring for a pair for yourself?"

Mr. Perkins shoes began to lead him away from the display. "Not really what I was thinking about finding today," he tried lamely.

He found himself edging off in another direction.

"Wait," Mrs. Mertz cried. "Mr. Perkins, please try on

those slippers." He turned toward her. "I'm going to pick up a pair for Homer and I want to see how you look in them."

He sat on the low bench but he couldn't remove his shoes. Not to be outdone by dominating shoes he summoned a deep breath and pulled harder. His face reddened, but for the life of him he couldn't get them off.

Mrs. Mertz sighed. "I want Homer to have a pair of shoes just like yours."

"Take them," Mr. Perkins gasped. "If you can get them off my feet, take them!"

"Oh, I could never do anything as selfish as that."

"Yes you could," he said. "Pull them off."

"I'm not that sort of woman." A tear brushed down the side of her cheek.

"No, really, please. Take them."

"I could never," she said.

"Why not? Can't you see I'm asking you?"

"But they fit you so perfectly," she ran her hand over his right shoe, shivered, and cupped it in her hands.

"They're perfect for Homer. Just pull them off."

She sighed. "I could never afford to pay you what you spent for them. Times are tough for all us these days Mr. Perkins."

"I only paid $7.00," he cried. "I've even got the slip to prove it."

She pulled away her hand. Her eyes narrowed and her lips pursed. "You mean to tell me…"

"Yes!" he pleaded.

"Then what's wrong with them?"

Homer Mertz joined them. He had two bags of new shoes. He looked like a kid with his first pair of Air Jordans. Mrs. Mertz pointed at Mr. Perkins' shoes.

"He said he only paid $7.00 for those." Her voice had a sharp edge.

"What's wrong with them, then?" Homer Mertz frowned. "Trying to fool us all, were you, Perkins?"

"What? What are you saying?" Mr. Perkins voice trembled.

"Wearing rich man's shoes. Trying to get us to think you're part of the one percent?"

"I- I- I never in my life!"

"Well, once fooled is one thing," Mertz said. He looked at his wife. "I think it's time you and I left." He looked at Mr. Perkins. "And you can forget about a seat on the Board."

"My car's at home," Mr. Perkins said.

"As far as I'm concerned, you and those phony millionaire shoes of yours can walk." Homer Mertz sneered and he and his wife huffed out of the store.

Mr. Perkins stared after them. "How will I get home?" he said, but the swinging doors had already swung shut behind Mr. and Mrs. Mertz.

He felt his shoes pull at him. The next thing he knew he was outside. He trudged through the parking lot, the exit road to Route 9, the green landscaping, and then to his surprise, his body lifted and floated upward. His shoes were clouds with wings. As he felt himself lifting, he closed his eyes. When he opened them he was standing on his street, right outside his house.

Lincoln's Desk

It was a typically busy morning at The White House. Carrying fresh bagels and coffee, the Chief of Staff joined the President in the Oval Office. Always observant, he looked quizzically at the antique mahogany desk and chair facing a window that overlooked the Potomac.

"Is there something I should know that we haven't discussed yet, like you renting out space in your office?"

The President smiled and took a bagel. He'd hoped no one would notice it, or at least think of the desk as little more than a historic relic. He cleared his throat. "This little experiment might confuse the public, so it's best to keep it quiet."

The Chief of Staff nodded. "Sure, we'll leave that desk to your biographers." He crossed his legs and sipped his coffee. "So, why's it in here?"

"So he can use it." The President said between bites.

"I gather that! But who?"

"Abraham Lincoln!" He stood and went over to it. Carefully, he removed the red Smithsonian tag from a brass drawer handle and slipped it into his pocket.

The Chief of Staff raised his eyebrows and tilted his head. "Why?"

"I thought he might like to use it," the President said.

"President Lincoln, you mean."

He nodded. "Remember all that commotion around

here last summer when Queen Elizabeth and Prince
Phil were here for their visit? She said FDR had
confided in her father that, ever since his assassination,
Lincoln's ghost walks these halls. I thought he'd like to
sit down and relax at his desk."

Despite his smile, the Chief of Staff was anything
but amused. He dreaded the potential worldwide
headlines: Tabloids screaming that his boss was sharing
the Oval Office with the ghost of Lincoln. He frowned.
"That's all the Republicans need."

"Not just Lincoln," the President went on.
"According to the Queen, the White House is riddled
with ghosts. She called it a sanctuary for dead
Presidents."

The Chief of Staff gulped his coffee and squirmed
in his chair. "Of course all has to be top secret!"

"Absolutely," the President agreed.

The Chief of Staff wrinkled his brow. "Does the
First Lady know about this?"

The President nodded. "Actually, this was all
Michelle's idea! She supervised getting it out of storage
and placed exactly where it stood before. She also made
sure that the stuff on the desk top is exactly as he left it
that fateful night."

"What about the press?"

"Executive Privilege!" the President smirked. He
remembered how often, during Watergate, Nixon had
repeated those words.

The Chief of Staff leaned back in his chair and
looked thoughtful. "I read once that the Thai people
believe ghosts may help out around the house. The
more members of the family accept their presence, the

more visible they become."

The President smiled. "Supposing he materializes and has a few well-chosen things to say on the Evening News."

"Republicans would have a field day!"

The President sighed. "You don't sound overly enthusiastic."

"Got that right," his Chief of Staff said as he stood to leave. "I'm not."

At lunch over three-cheese salami pizza the President shared that conversation with the First Lady.

She smiled. "Lincoln's desk's perfect over in that corner."

He nodded. "Michelle, we have to keep all this quiet."

Her eyebrows flared. "Why? What's the big deal?"

"If the voters find out, the '10 primaries could take a turn for the worse." He took a bite of pizza.

"There's that," she agreed. "But you've never backed down from trouble." She sipped at her water.

"Never invited it either," he said. "Remember the uproar when word got out that Nancy Reagan consulted an astrologer? That seems pretty tame by comparison."

"Every Republican woman inside the Beltway needed her astrological chart done in a hurry." Michelle giggled.

"Chief of Staff was adamant about our keeping this quiet. Tell the chef that was good pizza."

Michelle shook her head. "I will, but you ate too fast. How come you went and told him and now you're telling me not to talk about it."

"You know how insistent he can be. I told him what

the Queen said last summer."

"And?"

"He said she should switch from scotch to strong tea."

She shrugged and finished her pizza. "I'll never forget her expression when she told me how haunted this place really is. And if you want my personal opinion, I feel the American people have a right to know. They own this building, after all."

He shuddered. "No way! Look at the controversy something simple like Cash for Clunkers caused. Compared to that, this is huge."

She took his hand. "Bring it up in casual conversation next time my brother and his family come for dinner. See how they take it."

He frowned. "Knowing him, he'll tactfully suggest the pressure of the job's getting to me." He leaned in and gave her a kiss.

"Well I already told mama. She said if he happens to show up she wants to be there to shake his hand."

Across the room the portrait of President Garfield slid to one side.

The First Lady smiled. "Maybe he wants his old desk back in the Oval Office too."

"That's not funny."

"Well, you've always said you wanted your administration to be inclusive. Now's your chance."

It was past midnight when the ghost of Abraham Lincoln glided into the Oval Office. To his pleasure he discovered his desk and chair along with other personal belongings. His hand glided over his frayed appointment calendar and delicately touched the small leather bound Bible that had belonged to his wife, Mary Todd.

Most evenings it was his custom to float about the White House, dropping into various offices, reading memos and correspondence and absorbing dark chocolate from a particular workstation on the second floor. Sometimes he sampled the fine wines and liqueurs stored in the White House's wine cellar. Finally, sorrowfully he'd peruse each day's General Orders, and make note of the names of the dead who had fought so bravely in Afghanistan and Iraq. It grieved him and made him feel sad that all he could do was send light and prayers to their families and loved ones.

Much to his chagrin, aside from reading in the Library of Congress, there wasn't much that captured his interest. He still felt a natural reluctance to attend the theater; and aside from the sociality of infrequent pinochle games with the ghosts of Jim Garfield and Bill McKinley, both of whom inhabited the White House attic, or occasional visits to Georgetown hot spots with JFK, Abraham Lincoln's afterlife was solitary and often lonely.

But now hopefully his luck would change. Perhaps this newly elected young President, himself an attorney and constitutional scholar, might like to become his friend. He might even in some way wish to benefit from his wisdom and experience.

Gingerly, Abraham Lincoln sat down at his old desk. The tips of his bony fingers touched his quill pen, remarkably still intact along with other keepsakes that had been housed deep in the vaults of the Smithsonian.

He noticed his underlined copy of the Constitution was there too. Seeing it again helped him to remember with great joy that he was but one of forty-four Americans charged with preserving the dignity and clarity of that mighty document. Finally weary, his eyes closing, he leaned back in his old familiar office chair and went to sleep.

Early that next morning President Obama was busy at his desk systemically taking care of the enormous responsibilities that dogged his job. He sipped his coffee and bit into his toasted bagel. Then he sneezed.

"Bless you," came a soft gentle voice from the direction of the old desk. It seemed as ancient as time itself yet imbued with youthful vibrancy.

Momentarily startled the President turned in the direction of the desk. And then he smiled. "Is that you Abe? Abe Lincoln?"

Hearing his name repeated aloud, Lincoln began to materialize. At first the President saw a gray form that morphed into a glowing, evanescent presence. President Lincoln leaned back in his rickety desk chair, looked over at him and smiled back.

He spoke slowly. "I'm glad you took the time to read Thomas Paine's *Common Sense.*" His voice was deep and resonant, so close yet unfathomably distant.

"I did, that same night last summer while the Queen was here, when it fell from the bookcase. I kind of wondered how that happened. But I took it as a sign."

Lincoln nodded. "This democracy of ours is a tender child; it is our task and responsibility to afford it strength and to prevent from succeeding those eager to steal its heart away."

His eyes fixed on Abraham Lincoln, the President listened intently. Then for a brief moment a speck of doubt crossed his mind and clouded his vision. At that same moment Lincoln's image began to fade. Now all the President could see was a grayish misty shape in the long, lanky form of a man.

Lincoln's desk chair creaked back and forth. The old springs sounded like a string instrument in need of tuning. A soft voice hummed in the President's ears. "Thank you for returning my desk and personal belongings to me. That was very gracious."

The President nodded. "Feel free to use it anytime, anytime at all." He felt both amazed and highly self-conscious. "I'm always glad to chat with you, Abe. I'm sure your counsel could prove incredibly helpful to me." But there was no reply.

The President felt more than just a little discombobulated. The hairs on his arms bristled and his fingers felt icy cold. This connection with life after life was new for him. Feeling the same uncertainty his two young daughters had felt while they were getting used to the White House, he told himself what he had said to them: new places and new experiences take time to understand and feel comfortable.

He raised his voice. "Abe, Abe before you go just tell me one thing. Is there anything you'd like that I could do for you?"

Lincoln found himself smiling. This one was not like the others. This one was very special and the soft whisper of a "yes" floated on the air.

The President grabbed his yellow pad and pen. Before his eyes, Lincoln materialized, opened his palms and held them out toward him pleadingly.

"Bring the soldiers home, bring them home to their families. They are worn and tired and need the comfort of their loved ones..." Then his voice and presence faded and he was gone.

The President and the First Lady were sitting over lunch. "Just like that!" The First Lady said. She chomped down on her celery stick. "All he wants you to do is put an end to war." She laughed. "He's not asking for much now, is he? How are you supposed to do this? Go out in the middle of the field and blow a whistle like a referee at a football game? And that will make it all stop?"

The President picked at his salad." Would that I could," he sighed. He had little appetite. Looking up, he took her hand. "This whole thing is blowing my mind." He shook his head. "He looks just like he always did, hardly a gray hair." He laughed ruefully and ran his hands through his own.

The First Lady took his hand in both of hers. She looked into his eyes. "Perhaps this is part of a divine plan. Maybe President Lincoln has a real message for us all."

He laughed. "In that case he should share it with Joe Biden too. Then if Joe sees him like I do at least I'll know there's nothing weird going on in my head."

She smiled. "Of course something weird's going on. You're confronting a ghost; how strange is that?"

The Chief of Staff joined them. He hooked his foot around a wire chair and set a large steaming mug of coffee down on the small café table.

"Don't you ever eat lunch?" the First Lady asked. "All I ever see you do around meal time is drink coffee. The food here's pretty good, you know."

He smiled and looked at the President. "If I may speak candidly, you look like you've seen a ghost."

"That I have, and you know who it is too."

His face reddened. "Please keep it down. The last thing we need is for the press to get wind of these illusions of yours."

"I wouldn't call them that," the President said quietly.

"He isn't imagining anything," the First Lady added. "You can check it out yourself anytime."

The President waved his arm. "Call Joe Biden, get him over here right away."

His Chief of Staff shrugged and flipped open his cell phone. He looked at the First Lady. "You think it's real too?"

"Of course I do. I saw what happened to the Lincoln bedroom last summer during the Queen's visit. He got riled seeing a Union Jack bedspread on his bed and tore it to shreds. Plus, I've seen the portraits of Pierce and Garfield slide around on the walls trying to attract our attention."

The Chief of Staff grimaced. "Sorry I missed the show." He punched numbers into the phone.

"Tell him to meet us in the Oval Office." The President finished his coffee, kissed his wife and together they headed in that direction.

The Vice President, who had just returned from a fact-finding mission, was all smiles as he greeted the President, First Lady, and Chief of Staff."

"You're always smiling," the President said.

"What can I tell you? I'm in love with a gorgeous blond who just happens to be my wife. That good luck can make any man happy."

"Joe, I want you to be part of this." The President pointed toward the antique desk. "If Abe Lincoln appears he'll be right over there."

The VP blinked and flashed a look at the Chief of Staff and the First Lady. "What's all this about?"

"Joe, just relax," she said. "Suspend judgment and see what happens."

The Vice President shrugged. "Whatever you say."

"Sure, just watch the show," the Chief of Staff added.

"Abe," The President began. "Abe, are you here? I'm hoping we can speak with you."

Everyone waited nervously. The springs in the antique desk chair began to creak. Slowly, it rocked back and forth. A dark husky haze formed there.

Joe Biden peered at it. Then his eyes widened. "You're Abraham Lincoln!"

The misty presence coalesced and the tall figure of the murdered president became obvious. He smiled at Joe Biden. "It's always a pleasure to meet a man who keeps Scranton alive in his heart."

The Vice President gulped. "My privilege to meet you too, Sir."

"Abe," President Obama spoke. "Would you repeat for all of us what you said to me this morning?"

Abraham Lincoln smiled warmly. He held out his hands. "End war." His face sobered. "It is so unnecessary and so useless for the promotion of democracy." He sighed. "Instead, use those funds to afford compassion to the poor, especially the children. Our greatest hope lies with the young ones." Then he was silent.

After a pause the Vice President spoke. "Mr. President, I'm sure I speak for all of us here when I say I heartily agree with what you've just asked of us. If we could, we'd do that in a heartbeat. But to achieve the incredible change in policy you're suggesting we'd need the absolute cooperation of the Republicans, guys from your own party. Without them we can't rub two sticks together to light a campfire."

"Will you speak to them," the First Lady asked? "If we bring the minority leaders here to see you, will you face them and give them a good talking to."

Abraham Lincoln nodded. He smiled at the First Lady. "Yes," he said. "I'll be here." Then he sat back in his chair. It creaked a little and then fell silent. Slowly, he faded into the afternoon light.

The following morning the Chief of Staff and the President were conferring over coffee. "No way I can talk you out of this, is there?"

The President smiled. "Why *not* introduce Abe to the Republican leaders? We've nothing to lose. If they choose to be obstructive with the titular head of their own Party, then so be it."

"Republicans were pretty different back then."

"You think!" The President laughed." Politics always appears different depending upon the when of it, but it always remains the same too. Issues continually change but unfortunately war persists."

The Chief of Staff nodded. "Be a miracle if Lincoln could exert influence over his Party today." He finished his coffee and stood up. "Just so you know, I invited the Speaker to this afternoon's meeting."

"You did! Why?"

"Felt like a good idea. Sometimes a woman has a better handle on stuff like this."

After lunch Speaker of the House Nancy Pelosi, followed by the minority leaders of Congress along with Vice President Joe Biden and the First Lady, gathered in the Oval Office and seated themselves in the chairs placed facing Lincoln's desk.

The Speaker smiled at the President. "What a lovely piece of antique furniture. Are you initiating a new program? Cash for old desks?" She chuckled and nodded to the First Lady.

"Planning on having a yard sale Mr. President?" The Senate Minority leader smirked. "Sell off relics from the Smithsonian to help bring the deficit back down to earth?"

The President laughed. "Not a bad idea, but I couldn't sell that desk even if I wanted to. It doesn't belong to me. It's Abraham Lincoln's." He paused and cleared his throat. "The reason I called you here is that yesterday Joe Biden and I witnessed something astonishing. After careful consideration, we decided to share it with the Republican leadership."

Both minority leaders frowned.

The President continued. "During the Queen's visit she mentioned to Michelle and I that FDR had told her parents in confidence that the White House was haunted by ghosts of Presidents past. It seems that's still true. For obvious reasons this matter has been withheld from the press, and I implore your confidentially."

The House Minority leader rubbed his forehead and raked his fingers through what remained of his hair. He looked dubiously at the President. "And I suppose the next thing you'll tell us is that the ghost of Abraham Lincoln is sitting right over there."

The President nodded. "Got that right!"

The Speaker pointed toward the desk. "Yes! This may sound strange but I definitely feel some sort of presence there."

"Chalk one up to female intuition," Joe Biden chuckled.

The President leaned forward. "Abe? Abe Lincoln, are you here? I'd like you to materialize and talk to these folks I brought in to see you."

In the afternoon light, a hazy mist formed and hovered over the desk. Slowly the outline of Abraham Lincoln took shape and solidified.

No one said a word. From his desk chair, Lincoln nodded and began to speak. "Thank you for coming today. I will not take much of your time." He bowed to the Speaker. "My dear, did you know that Mrs. Lincoln always saw to it that I was never alone in my office with a woman?"

Her cheeks reddened. "Thank you for sharing that, Mr. Lincoln. This is the first time I've ever conversed with a ghost."

Lincoln smiled warmly. "Then we share a commonality. This is the first time I've ever conversed with a member of Congress who is a woman." He paused reflectively. "Even today women are still the last slaves."

"Some women," the First Lady interjected politely. "Not all of us, but yes, I hear you."

The House Minority Leader folded his arms across his chest. "Why are you here?"

Lincoln looked thoughtful. "I have a request: End all war. For the sake of the planet put an end to it as quickly as you can."

A buzz of conversation erupted. The House Minority leader turned toward President Obama. He shook his head and laughed. "Got to hand it to you Mr. President. You're a lot slicker than I thought. How'd you set this up anyway? This is like what my wife and I saw in that movie, *The Illusionist*."

Before the President could respond, the Senate Minority Leader jumped in. "Smoke and mirrors! Houdini baffled his audiences when he played games like this." He shook his head. "I must say, Mr. President, this ruse of yours almost had me fooled! And personally I'd nominate you for an Academy Award for special effects. Why not try it out on *Saturday Night Live?*"

The Vice President gripped the arms of his chair. "If you think we're trying to put something over on you, go on over there and check him out." But both men remained where they were. Lincoln's image began to grow transparent.

"Wait, please don't go," the Speaker pleaded. "I want to ask you something."

The House Minority Leader chuckled. "Who are you; some out of work actor? Play ball with us and we'll invite you to our National Convention. Show up in that get-up and you can deliver the Keynote Address. Imagine penciling Abraham Lincoln into the program!"

His colleague in the Senate guffawed. "That would give the delegates a real big rush now, wouldn't it!"

Speaker Nancy Pelosi addressed the shimmering form that hovered above Lincoln's desk chair. "How did you feel about continually having to deploy more and more troops during your Presidency?"

Lincoln's words resonated clearly: "Terrible! In hindsight, I've come to understand and appreciate General McClellan's reluctance to dispatch his men as swiftly as I had hoped." He looked about the Oval Office. "But I pray that any Chief Executive faced with such circumstances would be of sufficient mind to resist pressures to send our young to their graves."

The House Minority leader shook his head. "Never mind about our next National Convention, Abe—or whoever you are. We Republicans withdraw our invitation to be Keynote Speaker. We don't hold with those views."

President Obama looked intently at them. "You're both missing the point." The Vice President nodded in agreement.

The Senate Minority leader applauded. "Good show, Mr. President. "Like I said, these special effects you've concocted *are* worthy of an Academy Award."

The Speaker, however, concentrated intently upon Lincoln's wavering image. "Tell me," she asked, "is there a reason, with the world situation as it is, for you to ask that of us now?"

As he spoke his image momentarily grew stronger.

"There is only just so much pain a planet can endure and still remain in balance. There is a profound need now for all military activities to cease. I say this for the livelihood of our future generations, who deserve more than what the proliferation of war and its dire consequences could ever provide."

"Same kind of slop we heard during Viet Nam," the House Minority Leader said. He rose abruptly and pointed his finger at Lincoln. "You want our economy to crumble and throw everyone into chaos and despair worse than even during the Great Depression? You want to wipe hundreds of thousands of jobs right off the map? Well if you do, buddy, keep up that doomsday scenario of yours."

Lincoln's shape faded and became almost invisible. His words faded to a whisper: "But the alternative to proliferation is far worse."

The House Minority Leader stood and looked hard toward Lincoln's chair and then at President Obama. "Like I said, Mr. President, you put on a real good show. But to me this guy sounds even less like a Republican than Nelson Rockefeller ever did."

"Why do you say that?" the Speaker asked. "He makes perfect sense to me."

The Senate Minority Leader glared at her. "Were he really one of us he'd understand the value of military occupation." He turned toward Lincoln's desk. "There's more than just oil involved. Unless we stop terrorism from spreading, why…" he stammered, "like the ancient Romans, we'll be crushed under the yoke of barbarian oppression."

The Vice President jumped up. "Now hold on there! The Romans didn't have global warming, green house gases, or any other potential environmental disasters to consider."

The Senate Minority Leader shook his finger at the Vice President. "What you mean is they didn't have Al Gore getting in their way."

The President stood. He took a deep breath. "I didn't ask you here today to squabble, or to accuse me of trying to pull the wool over your eyes. My intent was to share this phenomenon in order that you Republicans might be included in this dialogue."

"Well, thank you, Mr. President," more than a hint of sarcasm was evident in the Senate Minority Leader's voice. "But we'll be going now. We have genuine business to legislate." The two moved toward the door.

The House Minority leader stopped and turned. "Don't worry, Mr. President, your little ruse is safe with us."

"No one would believe us anyway," his Senate colleague added as they left. "If we even hinted at the substance of this meeting they'd call us both loony tunes."

Nancy Pelosi shook her head and looked at the First Lady. "What's needed to convince those types is scientific proof that ghosts actually exist."

The First Lady nodded and smiled. "The problem is that most who demand proof are really only looking to disprove what they don't want to believe. I know that what we've seen here today is real."

The Speaker nodded and she and the Vice President stood and prepared to leave. The Vice President turned and saluted Lincoln's desk, "Just in case he's still here," he smiled.

The Speaker beamed. "Goodbye, President Lincoln. I want you to know that you're always a welcome guest in the House chambers despite the behavior of our Minority Leader." She and the Vice President left the Oval Office.

The President looked at the First Lady and took her hand. "Do you have to go too?"

"Only if you want your daughters fed supper."

"I'll be up in a bit," he smiled. "But first I want a few words with Abe."

They kissed and she left.

"You there, Abe?" the President asked. President Lincoln's tenuous form slowly reappeared. His kind eyes seemed sad. "I just want to say I hope we can still work together."

Abraham Lincoln nodded. "My friend, you have a long road ahead and many a weary night. I'll be near at hand."

"Thank you," the President replied. He sighed, stood, and left the Oval Office.

President Lincoln leaned back in his desk chair and smiled. "As I thought," he murmured, "this one is indeed different." Then he faded gradually from sight.

The Old TV

Helen saw it on the giveaway table at the Senior Center. In the realm of high tech it was ancient, a throwback to the nineteen fifties. The screen was less than ten inches. Though portable it was heavier than she had expected. But it did have a handle and the cord was intact. What clinched it for her was the leatherette finish that made it appear sporty.

Barney looked up as she came in their apartment. He chuckled. "What made you bring home that relic, Helen? You don't think it can be hooked up to our cable do you?"

"No need," she said sporting it like a new handbag. "It's the perfect size for my night table. When I can't sleep I can turn it on and if nothing else stare at the static."

"If you want a small TV, I can get you one that's equipped for cable and can play movies."

"I'm sorry if it bothers you," she said softly.

"It doesn't bother me," he smiled. "I just like to see my wife with up-to-date stuff."

"Why would you care how old something is?"

He thought about it. "I guess it makes me feel good to see you with new things. Like your cell phone, or the microwave you hardly ever want to use."

"I told you I don't trust microwaves." There was finality in her voice.

"We can afford something better." He made his point. Now the jury could deliberate.

She laughed. "Well, if you feel that way, let's take a three-month cruise around the world. We've always talked about doing that."

He sat up and she could tell he was getting his thinking in order. Then he said. "A new laptop with a TV card is a lot less expensive than an around-the-world cruise."

That made her smile. "Barney, for the last twenty years you'd say anything imaginable was a lot cheaper than sailing anywhere romantic."

"There are pirates in the South Seas, Helen." She knew he had justified his position, so why bother talking? She went over to him and kissed him. "Well, if you change your mind and feel romantic, I'll be in the bedroom watching my new TV."

She plugged it in under her night table. The cord reached and she felt a bolt of happiness when she saw how nice the leatherette design looked next to her array of meds. Might as well face reality and turn it on she said to herself. She wondered if anything would come through.

The static sounded like an old drunk coughing. Then the snow gave way to wavy lines that were almost hypnotic. She remembered she was eight when her parents bought one of the first TV's. Then, on the screen, she saw her friend, Sarah. *That seems strange.*

"Did I tell you what Helen told me the other day?" Sarah said. She was talking about her. *What on earth?*

Then she saw Jennifer, Sarah's friend who lived with her. "That scatterbrain," Jennifer chuckled. "Who cares what she says?"

Helen felt angry, betrayed, confused. She fidgeted with her wedding ring and tears sprang out of nowhere. Abruptly she changed the channel. The loud, drunken belching startled her, then came snow and more black wavy lines. On the screen she saw Tom and Elsie in their living room. Tom was unbuttoning her blouse. Elsie didn't seem to mind. She laughed and kissed her husband of forty years. Helen felt embarrassed, as though she were intruding, and quickly turned off the TV.

Barney came into the bedroom. He saw she was crying. He put his arm around her shoulders. "What's the matter?"

She shook and began to stammer. "Jennifer said mean things about me."

He shrugged. "She talks that way about everyone. That's why people stay away from her at church, except Sarah, who in my estimation is a saint for putting up with her. Who told you?"

Now she was flustered. "Nobody. I heard her on the TV?"

He cracked a grin. "You soused?"

She took a deep breath. "Never mind. Forget it. I shouldn't have said anything. I know things like that aren't supposed to happen."

"So who told you, anyway?" He went to his bureau and found his nail clip.

She pointed to the TV. "If you must know," she said. "I saw them on that."

"You out of your mind?"

She clenched her jaw. "Just once," she sobbed,

"you're going to listen to what I say without making me feel like an idiot. See for yourself." She moved away from the bed. "Go ahead. Turn it on."

"I'll do anything you want. But please stop crying. You know how that makes me feel." Reluctantly he went to the TV and flipped the switch. He saw the snow followed by the wavy lines and then the hacking and coughing started. He looked at her and when he looked back at the screen Ernie and Jake were playing gin in Ernie's family room.

He peered at the screen. Surprise and amazement spread across his face like a forest fire.

Helen drew closer. As he reached to turn it off she heard: "You think Barney will go to the track with us on Saturday?" Jake said.

"Doubtful," Ernie mumbled. "Lost five bills the last time. Probably didn't even tell his wife."

Between Here and There

Harry never thought much about the hereafter or whatever they called life after death. The whole idea of reincarnation seemed far-fetched to him—the subject of Broadway musicals perhaps, but certainly not anything to be taken seriously.

In his last moments of life, he saw the face of a nurse holding a damp cloth to his forehead. His entire body was numb. Despite the pain medication, his chest burned. He stared at her. Then everything faded.

The next thing he knew he was wearing a fancy, embroidered gold robe, standing in the middle of a posh hotel lobby. A sign flashing "This Way to the Dining Room" pointed down a corridor.

Harry didn't feel particularly hungry. He began to take in his surroundings.

"Hi! You must be Harry. Welcome! We've been expecting you, and we hope everything is satisfactory."

An attractive young woman stood beside him. Her blond hair curled around her shoulders. Her eyes were bright blue. She was fashionably dressed, like a hostess in a posh restaurant.

Harry felt confused. "What's happening? Am I dead? Or is this some kind of dream and I'll wake up back in the hospital?"

She nodded, took his hand gently and smiled. "This is no dream. You're here. You have died." She squeezed his hand excitedly. "See, it's nothing like anyone ever expects. It's really just a world within a world within a world, and so on and so forth."

"That sounds poetic," he sighed, and for a moment realized how limber and young he felt. He looked around. The upholstered sofas and chairs seemed familiar, the same furnishings his parents might have had. Beautiful paintings like the ones he had in his gallery hung on the walls. He'd owned an art gallery on Park Avenue that catered to the rich and famous, and it had made him a good living.

In the center of the lobby was an atrium that held an inviting garden filled with trees and blooming flowers. In the midst of it a beautiful fountain chimed as it sprayed effervescent golden sparkles of light high into the air.

Harry stared at his surroundings. She stood beside him.

"None of this seems particularly Biblical. I guess I expected someplace that looked more like clouds and angels and less like the lobby of the Ritz Carlton."

She nodded and gently touched his cheek. "Of course not," she said. "Do you think people would remain content with their earthly time if they knew that what was waiting beyond their comprehension was so special? But please, relax. And don't be in any rush to go to the fountain."

"And you're an angel?" She had the most beautifully innocent face.

She smiled. "That angelic stuff— you know, wings, long flowing white robes? All that was made popular by artists during the Renaissance and by now is passé." She looked deeply into his eyes and smiled. "I'm what you'd call a hospitality hostess. At least that's what it says on my job description." She handed Harry a small bag of candy.

"What's this for?"

"Your pleasure, enjoy a piece or two and see."

He tasted one and smiled. A warm feeling of love washed over him.

He looked at her. It seemed for an instant he saw his mother's face, and other faces of women he had known when he was young. She smiled again and patted his hand. "We hope you're pleased and comfortable."

"Oh, you mean this is where I get to stay?" That idea felt very comforting and slowly where he was began making sense to him. From the bag he took another candy.

"Everyone has his or her own suite," she said. "Yours is near the golf course."

"This is wonderful. I feel so happy, just like I'm a little kid." He giggled. The fountain sang behind him. He turned toward it.

"You are," she hugged him. "Doesn't it feel wonderful to be that way again?"

"What's with the fountain? Why did you say what you did about it?"

"You don't have to go there yet. You can spend your time relaxing here." She took his hand. "What could be better than that?"

"What could?" Was it his mother's voice? Those were her words. She always said that. He gazed at her. Her face seemed to change, reflecting familiar faces, all of them loving and touching his heart.

"I feel like I'm young again. But that couldn't be. Could it?"

"What do you think? Only you can answer that for yourself. Only you can know." She touched his heart.

He raised his arms upward and smiled. "I want to be young and strong. I want to start out again, living life."

"Yes," she said. "You can."

As she released his hand he felt drawn once more toward the fountain. As he approached it he felt embraced by feelings of love so intense he was captivated by joy. He was swept into the golden mist. He felt deliriously loved and happy.

His blurry vision cleared. He was wrapped in something soft. A smiling woman was holding him close. She beamed at the man beside her bed. As Harry drifted off to sleep he felt content and happy.

She cuddled the infant. "Look, he's got Uncle Harry's smile."

The man nodded and gently put his arm around his wife's shoulders. "Our son," he said.

The Book

"Is this book really only a dollar?" Jeffrey asked the volunteer at the library book sale. He held out a small volume, bound in leather with an odd red and blue design on the cover.

The volunteer took it and nodded. She looked through the thick, crinkly pages and handed it back. "Yes. Oddly, this title keeps turning up at our book sales."

"Great!" He handed her the dollar and left. Outside, though it was sunny and mild, he felt a sudden chill. He hurried home with his prize where he examined it more carefully. It was printed in a script he couldn't recognize. The illustrations depicted strange looking people, some of whom seemed vaguely familiar.

He looked at the cover again. Embedded into the leather was a thin slice of iridescent blue stone. He sighed. "This book must be purely ornamental," he said.

Hungry, he made himself a late lunch. The fish and vegetables were fresh, yet they seemed tasteless. The wedge of blueberry pie baked by his neighbor had no flavor.

He cleared away his plates and began to wash them. As he looked up from the sink, he noticed that his kitchen walls had taken on a grayish hue. He felt weary. *Perhaps I need a nap*, he thought. He went into his normally bright bedroom. The colors seemed faded. Everything appeared lusterless.

He lay down on his bed and dozed off. When he woke, the sky had darkened. Even after he turned on the lamp the bedroom looked dull. He went into the kitchen, opened the refrigerator and peered at the remains of the gray, unappetizing blueberry pie. What could be wrong with him?

He made himself a fresh cup of coffee and poured it into a cup. The coffee had no aroma or flavor. *Something strange is going on*, he thought.

He called his doctor and told him his symptoms.

"Has this happened before?" his doctor asked.

"No," Jeffery said.

The doctor's voice was offhand. "Possibly the flu or a virus. Take two aspirins and call me in the morning if this condition persists."

"It hit me out of nowhere."

"Could even be an allergy; mold, house dust. Might have been brought on by anything."

As he concluded the conversation, the numbers on his phone blurred so that he could hardly see them. He went into his living room and turned on the TV. Even with the volume up higher than usual he could barely hear, let alone see, much of anything except a dim pallor and faded shapes moving about the screen but making little sense.

A sudden rain battered the windowpanes. Lightning and thunder cracked through the sky. Oddly, he felt isolated and alone. Usually he was happy to be here, surrounded by his books and his memorabilia. Now the whole room seemed damp and foggy. He tried to turn on the floor lamp beside his chair. It didn't light. Had the bulb burnt out? However, the light switch didn't work either. He tried other lamps in the house. With a flashlight he checked his circuit board. Puzzled, he picked up the phone to call the electric company. The phone was dead.

His head began to whirl and he sat down. Now he was too dizzy to even try to get out of his chair. His breath was diminishing. He felt a weight on his chest. *Could I be dying?* he thought.

Jeffery had never considered his own demise. He was a young man in his late thirties; strong, energetic, sociable, and according to his doctor, very healthy. This morning as he had walked to the library book sale he had felt wonderfully buoyant: optimistic, hopeful of discovering a unique collectible to show to his antiquarian book collector friends.

His mind worked only slowly. He probed his memory for clues. All he could think of was the book he had just brought home; the curious odd volume with the words he couldn't read.

He reached for it and tried to lift it. It seemed very heavy. It had hardly weighed anything when he had first picked it up. With an effort that left him exhausted he pulled the book onto his lap.

Now the pages opened on their own. They turned to illustrations of people who somehow seemed familiar, people he used to know in town but never saw any more. The last image resembled a man whose body was twisted and squashed down into itself. Its face frighteningly resembled his own.

Speechless, he felt trapped. He needed to do something. His mind wouldn't move beyond its thick fog of confusion.

Dimly, he recognized that the book must have

something to do with this. He tried to push it away, but it stayed on his lap. He felt weaker; energy slipped away from him. As he fell back in his chair, his eyes lit on the illustration that resembled him. It was now in full color, and the face, his face, was contorted into an expression of utter despair.

After his funeral, his next of kin cleared out his house. His books were boxed up and donated to the library. At the next book sale the odd volume bound in leather reappeared on the dollar table awaiting the next bibliophile to take it home, pleased that he or she had uncovered a rare treasure.

Mr. Perkins and the Wee Folk

Mr. Perkins felt uncomfortable whenever the subject of anything even remotely mystical came up. He considered himself rational; he preferred man-to-man talk about accounting procedures or, if need be, lawn and garden care. He was then surprised when, at a recent church supper, Bess Smothers asked him if he'd ever met any of the Wee Folk face to face.

"That's a new thought," Mr. Perkins squirmed.

"We're going tomorrow night! Come with us, Henry!"

"Going where and why?"

"To see the Wee Folk," she said. "They're helpful, and I think it's time more people from church knew about them."

He wondered if she had been drinking. "Where are they?"

"All around us, I'd guess." She chuckled. "That's what makes finding them so easy. They find us."

"Are you trying to tell me that there are Wee Folk all around me that I can't see?"

"Yes," she smiled. "Oh good, you understand."

Poppycock, he thought. What was wrong with this woman anyway? Did she really expect him to believe this? He merely smiled and said. "Oh, really…" He and his departed wife knew the Smothers well. They even sat together at church on Christmas Eve. But he couldn't imagine either woman ever discussing anything like this."

"I thought you knew," she sighed. ""Helen and I practically discovered them together."

He cleared his throat. This was preposterous. She had to be intoxicated. "You're saying you and Helen…"

"Yes," she said. "One of them helped her find her grandfather's watch that was lost in your attic."

That took him aback. "Yes! I remember when she found it."

"Or when she found your car keys for you. Apparently you were always misplacing them."

His face reddened. This revelation was true. "And you're saying it was these Wee Folk who led her to my keys?"

"And the lottery wins too," Bess Smothers said. "Remember when she'd come home with winning fifty dollar scratch tickets?"

"Yes!" His breath thumped in his chest and he had the sense that something of Biblical proportions had been revealed to him.

Before he had a chance to think: "Good! Then it's settled. I'll pick you up tomorrow night at seven."

"When you put it that way," he sighed, something about this conversation felt lunatic to him. He lowered his voice. "I do consider myself a bit of a free thinker."

That next evening, Mr. Perkins climbed into Bess Smothers' mini-van. He was greeted by hearty voices and smiling faces.

"What's the plan?" Brad Hopkins asked. He wore a Red Sox cap that slipped over his ears.

"I brought them some grapes," Marge Bovus said. "Hi, Henry."

"Oh, they'll like that," Bess said.

"What did you bring, Henry?" Marge asked.

"Bring? I didn't know I was supposed to bring anything." Mr. Perkins said. Reluctantly he reached down into his pants pockets but only touched his keys and his lucky half dollar.

"We always bring an offering," Brad said. "Makes them happy and we end up with more in the end."

Mr. Perkins eyed him suspiciously. "You've been doing this awhile, Brad?"

"Every chance I get," he said. He pulled the cap up and fiddled with the brim. "This one's two sizes too big. Was all they had in stock."

"Why?" Mr. Perkins asked. "Red Sox caps can be pricey."

"Last time I did, when I got home there were box seats for the White Sox series waiting for me on my desk."

Mr. Perkins wondered if Brad needed tranquilizers.

Marge pointed off to the right. "Turn up there."

Bess turned her mini-van onto a bumpy dirt road. Mr. Perkins felt like he was in the middle of nowhere. Nervously he said, "No lights anywhere."

"That's a good sign," Brad said.

As though on cue Bess pulled up and parked. Everyone climbed out. They were standing in a farmer's field.

"This could be private property," Mr. Perkins said.

"Usually how it is these days," Brad said.

Bess Smothers lit a green candle and placed it on the hood. Then she lit a decidedly sweet smelling stick of incense. "Let's form a circle like we did last time."

Mr. Perkins didn't understand why he was holding hands with them all in a muddy field. Then he heard childlike giggling interspersed with indecipherable chatter. He wondered, *were these the same Wee Folk who had put Rip Van Winkle to sleep for all those years?* All he could think was, *oh what have I gotten myself into?*

"We're here," Bess Smothers said cheerfully. "Let's get closer in the circle," she urged the others.

"We've all brought gifts," Marge said. "Would you like them now?"

"Take me out to the ball game," Brad sang.

To Mr. Perkins it sounded like they were talking to little children.

Bess and Marge reached into their handbags and tossed pocket change onto the ground. Brad pulled several ball point pens from his jacket, put them into the Red Sox cap and placed it by his feet.

All Mr. Perkins could possibly contribute was either his house keys, which was preposterous, or his lucky half dollar from the Columbian Exhibition of 1892. It had belonged to his grandfather. He'd been given it as a boy. He didn't want to give it up. What he wanted to do was to go sit in the mini-van and wait for the others to be ready to go home.

Bess Smothers noticed Mr. Perkins edging away from the circle. "Oh no, Henry, you mustn't do that. You can't break the circle or you'll spoil everything."

She had a flustered shrill in her voice that always made him nervous. When a woman's voice took him by surprise like that, he'd freeze, unable to function.

Bess touched his arm. "Tell us Henry, what's the matter?"

The incense had stuffed up his nose. "I really haven't anything to give them." He was flustered, pierced by the horns of a dilemma beyond his control.

"Oh come now, dear." She took his hand and squeezed it the same way his mother had when he was little and got upset.

"I'm really fine, thank you. Just go on with whatever you are doing without me. I'll stand here."

Marge turned toward him. "But why, Henry?" From the corner of his eye he could see two slight forms playing leapfrog.

"It's personal," he said, hopeful that that was sufficient.

Brad looked over at him. "I guess it's just a matter of trusting what feels right inside you. After that, you're home free." He grinned into the darkness.

Mr. Perkins sensed something decidedly odd about all of them, but what?

"All that I have with me is a family treasure that belonged to my grandfather; his fifty cent piece from the Columbian Exposition of 1892. I've carried it in my pocket since I was a small boy."

"Maybe it's time you gave it away then," Brad said.

"I don't want to! And were I to give it away one day, I wouldn't just toss it in this muddy field and lose it. I'd hand it down and keep it in the family."

"I'm sure we all understand how you feel," Bess said. Her patronizing tone reminded him of his grade school teachers.

Now embarrassment climbed over the horror of this situation.

"But you wouldn't be throwing it away, Dear," Bess said. "You'd be giving it to the Wee Folk. That's entirely different. They are so generous and kind to us."

He heard laughter and the gibber of high-pitched musical conversation. Then Brad laughed heartedly and Marge and Bess shook their hands in the air like schoolgirls playing Ring Around the Rosie.

"You don't have to decide anything, really," Bess said. "Just stay in the circle." She guided his shoulder closer to them.

The scent of the sage incense was evident. Everyone's cheeks were red and they all swayed and giggled.

"Smile, Henry," Bess said. "All it takes is a smile. Simple gifts are joyous gifts."

But Mr. Perkins didn't want to smile. He felt he had the right not to feel good if that meant having to toss away his grandfather's silver coin.

He caught a glimpse of a wee person who looked a little like a leprechaun from pictures he'd seen in books as a boy. It was small enough to fit in the palm of Bess Smothers hand. Her face radiated happiness. She handed him a small feather.

The leprechaun took the feather and waved it over Bess' nose. She sneezed and below her lay a dozen eggs.

"Thank you," she bent down to pick them up. Carefully she put them in the cooler. "Magical eggs from over the rainbow," she laughed. They all started humming "Over the Rainbow."

A whimsical looking leprechaun landed on Mr. Perkins right arm just below his shoulder. He fixed Mr. Perkins in his gaze and smiled mischievously.

Mr. Perkins face reddened, but for a moment he felt incredibly young. Without even thinking about what he was doing, he reached into his pants pocket and clasped his lucky coin. Then he handed it to the leprechaun.

The next moment it vanished into thin air.

High in the sky a crow cawed. Mr. Perkins was jolted back into himself. Immediately he reached into his pocket. "It's gone. My grandfather's silver coin, gone!" Tears sprang to his eyes.

This was not eggs in return for a feather. This was nothing. He felt cheated and robbed. He deserved better than this. He had always given at work whenever asked. He dropped to his knees and reached around trying to find his coin.

"Get a grip on yourself, Henry." Bess Smothers said. "It's not there."

"It has to be. That's where it landed when it fell out of my hand."

"But it didn't fall. You handed it to one of the Wee Folk. That's what we all saw." Marge said.

"Yes," Bess agreed.

Brad's face was suffused with joy and he was humming softly to himself.

Mr. Perkins felt shaken. If what they said was true, what he was saying made no sense, so why was he saying it? This confused him even more, and all he wanted was to go home.

As they climbed back into Bess' mini-van, he felt discouraged and sad. They drove home in silence.

He staggered into his house. How could he have been so foolish? He had allowed himself to be duped, and he had lost his boyhood treasure. How could he have done that?

He walked into his bedroom, turned on the light, and started getting ready for bed. He went to his bureau to get his pajamas. There sitting on the top were ten shiny Columbus Exposition silver half-dollars, all dated 1892.

The Dreadful

A gigantic dark slug, the Dreadful, lived in the town sewer. Measuring nearly twenty yards long, when it sought sustenance it crawled from the sewer into the pipes beneath the old gray building at the senior housing complex. There it devoured grease and sludge. Occasionally it would crawl out onto the parking lot from a wide opening hidden by shrubbery.

Many of the older residents knew of the Dreadful but hesitated to speak of it, even amongst themselves. Anyone who had mentioned it to the staff was instantly hospitalized and experienced painful electro-shock intended to cure obvious delusions. While the Dreadful never attacked a resident, its mere presence was frightening. This was especially true when, at dusk, it crawled out through the opening and slithered across the parking lot to devour various vehicles.

No one really knew what the Dreadful was except that it lived, hissed, bore frightening fangs, and contained a mouth that could swallow anything from a late-model Chevrolet to a refrigerator truck packed full of beer. Every night it would crawl through the pipes, its destination random, its senses responding to the arrival of fresh grease and sludge.

Two residents, Betty Sloan and Elvira Middlemarch, stood on their third floor porch and watched as the Dreadful devoured a recreational vehicle.

"That will cause a ruckus," Betty said.

Elvira nodded. "I know. It belongs to the Superintendent. He only just got it." At that moment the Dreadful spat up a fender and a GPS not to its liking.

Betty sighed. "He'll blame us all and threaten to raise our rents."

"I'm sure they'll throw the book at us at the next meeting," Elvira giggled as the Dreadful burped what smelled like gasoline and then, under the cover of darkness, slithered out of sight. "I wonder if it can think or has any idea what it's doing?"

"Remember when it swallowed the Head Nurse's Chrysler?" Betty said.

"And then fairly recently when it swallowed the Chief Psychologist's Toyota."

Elvira nodded. 'Imagine his blaming us and insisting the police check our fingerprints. Really! And then saying one of us had it stolen as some kind of vendetta."

Betty nodded. "At our age, everything's harder to distinguish when it's twilight and things blend into the shadows. Some can see it and some cannot. I remember Bess and Rudolph walked right past it early one evening without even noticing it." Betty took her notepad pad out from her corduroy jacket pocket and jotted down its swallowing the RV. Without telling anyone, she had always felt a sort of odd kinship with the Dreadful, and she meticulously documented everything she could about it. She considered herself its official biographer.

The morning after the RV had been devoured the Head Nurse called a mandatory meeting of all residents in the common room for later that evening. Like the Chief Psychologist, she was certain that discontented residents were responsible for these auto thefts.

"Vengeful geriatrics!" the Chief Psychologist said, frosted that his prized Toyota had no doubt been taken apart somewhere in a South Boston chop shop.

"Use any force necessary," the Director told the Chief Nurse.

It was a hot, humid night. From the opening the Dreadful watched attentively.

"The residents must be keeping something from us," the Director said.

"I wouldn't worry about that," the Head Nurse said. "Our Chief Psychologist knows how to reach inside their minds and extract even what they have long since forgotten."

"Surely that's nothing like a lobotomy," he sounded tense.

She eyed him strangely. "Using only government-approved methods."

Nervously, the residents gathered and sat down on hard, folding chairs in common room. The Director, Head Nurse, and Chief Psychologist along with two policemen sat facing them from a podium.

The Chief Psychologist cleared his throat. "We know you know. I suggest you make it easy on yourselves and tell us."

"One of you has to know something," the burly policeman said.

"We're all family here," the Director tried to smile. He looked to the Chief Nurse, a large grotesque woman with several chins and exceptionally large feet. She shook her fist and shouted, "If you know what's good for you, you'll tell us what you know about these vehicle thefts."

No one said a word.

"We're warning you," the Chief Psychologist and the Head Nurse both glared at the cowering residents.

"Don't you think they'd have figured it out by this time?" Elvira whispered.

Betty shrugged. "Don't bet on it." Bravely she stood up. "Look in the opening behind the bushes by the gray building."

Casting her a disdainful glance, the Director, the Chief Psychologist and the Head Nurse stood up and marched out.

Shortly thereafter a long, low series of screams pierced the night air. Lights flickered across the complex, glass shattered, several mournful cries rang out, and then silence. Betty took out her ballpoint pen and jotted a few words on her notepad.

The policemen drew their guns and exited cautiously.

After several minutes of silence the residents slowly returned to their apartments. The newer ones had no idea what had happened. Older ones knew only too well.

Later that month a new and more amiable Director, Head Nurse and Chief Psychologist were appointed to the jobs vacated by their predecessors, who had disappeared the night of the meeting, never to be seen again.

It was the night of the full moon. Crouched deep within the recesses of the sewer beneath the old gray building at the senior housing complex, the Dreadful awoke and howled. From inside the buildings, the distant sound resembled the cumbersome passing of a freight train.

Dreadful was seized by an overwhelming hunger. The dark slug howled again and again, slithering forward past the larger sewer pipes and eventually toward the faint glimmer of light leading to the knoll and shrubbery adjacent to the parking lot.

Betty Sloan and Elvira Middlemarch sat together on their shared porch. "Do you think?" Betty peered at the cars and then at Elvira.

The sound of loud abrasive metallic scraping persisted. "Look!" She pointed to the back row of the lot where a classic orange Volkswagen Beetle swirled in the air until it was swallowed up into a long dark snout.

Elvira sighed. "It gets noisy that way when it's hungry." Her hand brushed against her soft blue curls. "I guess we'd act noisy too if we were hungry."

Betty nodded. "But shouldn't we do something? It isn't right not to. After all, we're witnesses."

"And you remember what happened the last time we said anything? We tried. We spoke up at the tenants meeting, and when they went outside to check, the Director, Head Nurse and Chief Psychologist vanished without a trace."

"Even so, we can't pretend nothing's going on. We know something is. Look!" She pointed as a shiny silver Toyota was twirled and smashed against the concrete before chunks of it were devoured.

The following morning the new Chief Psychologist had barely checked his email when a staff person ushered Betty and Elvira into his office. Outside, the State Police CSI unit was busy; the parking lot, filled with official trucks, was cordoned off. Dislodged concrete was haphazardly flung onto a number of parked vehicles. Small, chewed chunks of Volkswagen and Toyota cluttered a small patch of lawn adjacent to the shrubbery.

"And how are you ladies doing today?" the new Chief Psychologist smiled.

"We've come to say what we saw." Elvira said.

"Last night," Betty said.

He smiled and nodded. "Yes."

Elvira looked down at her hands. "We saw it, but we can't explain exactly what it was we saw."

Betty nodded in agreement.

"Then you saw something unexplainable?"

"Yes, that's about it." Betty seemed confused.

"It had to be alive," Elvira said with certainty.

"Yes." The Chief Psychologist sat back in his chair. "Sometimes we think we see things that aren't really there at all." His voice sounded soft and his words were carefully chosen and deliberate. "What was it you think you saw?"

"But that's just it," Elvira said. "It's hard to describe something you've never seen before. It did have a long snout like an elephant's trunk and it slithered like a snake."

"That's for sure." Betty said.

"A trunk like an elephant that slithers like a snake." He tried envisioning something that fit that description only to feel perplexed.

"It must have been hungry," Betty said.

Finally Elvira smiled. "I guess it has a mind of its own when it comes to deciding what it wants to eat. Wouldn't you say?"

"Well, that's a good thing then," the Chief Psychologist said. "I want to thank you both for sharing what you saw with me. I'll be certain to get back to both of you."

"You don't think we're bonkers or anything like that, do you?" Elvira said at the door.

"Of course not!" He smiled. "Lots of us think we see strange sights like that." His voice remained gentle and soft. "Why, long ago as a boy I used to think I saw gigantic bugs."

"Maybe you did," Elvira said.

"Then it's not just us," Betty said.

"Happens all the time," he assured them. "Now, don't let something like that spoil your lunch."

"But we saw it eat the cars," Betty said.

He nodded and smiled. "We'll be in touch." His voice was as smooth and bland as skim milk.

Minutes later he was in the parking lot. Much of it looked like it had been hit by a tornado. He approached the State Police Sergeant. "Any luck?"

Reluctantly, the Sergeant shook his head. "Haven't figured it out yet. Vandalism if you ask me."

"Two of our residents told me that last night they saw something moving around back there. They said it had a long trunk like an elephant and slithered around like a snake."

The Sergeant's face reddened. "You don't expect me

to tell something like that to my Captain, now do you?"

"I thought I'd best let you know."

"Next thing you'll say is that it came out of nowhere and gobbled up those vehicles like some sort of hungry mutant."

The Chief Psychologist nodded. "Could be. Just thought I'd let you know."

"Thanks," the Sergeant said curtly. "Now if you don't mind I've got a crime scene to investigate. This is a case of vandalism; kids probably. We'll post a couple of men. If they come back tonight, we'll have them behind bars by morning."

The following morning the Sergeant arrived to discover that all that remained of his men were several mismatched shoes, a broken billy club, and a badly-gnawed cell phone.

The following morning at State Police Headquarters, the Commander called the Captain and Sergeant to a meeting. Both seemed bewildered as to exactly what had happened in the parking lot at the senior housing complex the previous night. His frown lines deepened as he studied the photographs of all that remained from the stake out operation.

"This might have been some kind of mob hit," the Commander conjectured. "Who's in that old age home? Anyone from the Witness Protection Program?"

"We've checked out the residents," the Sergeant said efficiently. "All good folk. No shady pasts."

The Commander's face reddened. "I don't buy that

adolescent vandal theory! Have either of you ever known a kid able to snap a billy club in two or chew a cell phone?"

"No," the Captain replied. "But kids are different today."

"Supposing you both try explaining what's going on!"

The Sergeant cleared his throat. "According to the Chief Psychologist at the housing complex, an elderly resident named Elvira Middlemarch told him that she saw some sort of creature with a long snout like an elephant's trunk that slithered like a snake across the parking lot."

The Captain looked askance at the Sergeant. "And I suppose the next thing you'll tell me is that little green men in space ships landed there."

"No, sir!" the Sergeant's face reddened. "There was no mention of little green men."

The Commander tried unsuccessfully to imagine a slithering elephant snout chewing on a cell phone. He frowned and shook his head sadly. "Sergeant, what you just said sounds like the kind of science fiction I remember reading as a kid." He stood and walked to the window.

"In the unlikely event that something like that actually exists, I'm ordering a swat team assembled and put into position." He clenched his fists. "If some weirdo from outer space wants to take on the Massachusetts State Police, then bring it on!" He walked back to his desk and eyed his two subordinates. "We'll use maximum force and blast whatever this is to smithereens."

The Captain interjected. "But sir, isn't it possible that this incident might emanate from some sort of harmless college fraternity prank? A hoax perpetrated by the students intending to make a big splash on YouTube or Facebook? I'd sure hate to see us make a mistake and decimate some techie college kids using maximum force."

The State Police Commander nodded. "Both of you get over to that housing complex and talk to this Middlemarch woman. Make sure all of her marbles line up the right way. I don't want us played for fools either. Just to be on the safe side, I'm ordering a 24/7 total media blackout on this case until further notice. No press! No TV! Absolutely nothing revealed to any sources until we see a clear playing field."

"Or an empty parking lot," the Sergeant said.

The Head Honcho of *Moment-to-Moment TV News* read the media gag order and immediately called a meeting of his senior staff. "Something's going on at that senior housing complex and I want our viewers to know what it is."

"Vandals," the News Editor said. "I've already read the initial report from the State Police. Probably kids acting up. Maybe shooting off fireworks."

The Head Honcho waved the media gag order as though it were a declaration of war. "I'm not so sure! Something about this whole business just doesn't smell right to me, and I've learned that, to survive in the news business, you need to trust your sense of smell to get things right. A good story has to have that perfect smell of..." he paused and rolled his eyes, "freshly brewed coffee, or even a bouquet of roses. I trust my nose to know that something stinks to high heaven."

"Like something's rotten in Denmark," the anchor for the Evening News said. "Let me go over there with a film crew and check it out."

"Sorry Lydia, but you're already slated to cover the Quahog Festival in Hyannis. Can't let our sponsors on the Cape down."

"Apparently the State Police posted a stake out last night," the News Editor said. "Something extraordinary must have happened for them to issue this sort of gag order."

The Head Honcho's face reddened. He stood up from his desk. "Alert all our affiliates: New York, DC, LA, London, Paris, even Rome. See if the Vatican has something to say. Even a 'no comment' from the Pontiff can be shaped into big news." He pulled at his nose and looked directly at his news editor. "From now on give this story your highest priority and your full attention. I want the world to know what's going on."

Outside, the day grew warmer. Inside, deep within the large sewer pipe, the Dreadful yawned. It slurped the last few drops of motor oil from the twisted chassis of the Toyota. The combination of oil mixed with thick black sewage grease was all it required for sustenance. Without it, it would slowly grow more and more irritable, until at last unable to control its hunger, it would emerge from its lair to hunt again.

The Captain and Sergeant walked up the metal stairs in the senior housing complex to Betty and Elvira's shared apartment. The Sergeant knocked, and Betty opened the door.

She recoiled nervously at the sight of his uniform. "Are you here to arrest us?" Elvira sat quietly in her easy chair by the window.

The Sergeant smiled. "Now why would we be thinking to do something like that to two such lovely ladies as you?"

"But we would appreciate your sharing with us what you know about the occurrences here," the Captain said.

Betty frowned. "The former Director, the Chief Psychologist and the head Nurse went to investigate outside."

"And they vanished, like they were just swallowed up," Elvira said.

The two men looked perplexed. "What's this? I came about the cars," said the Captain. "What can you tell me about what happened to the cars?"

"None of the residents dare say anything about seeing it."

"What?" the Sergeant asked.

Betty's face paled. "We're all afraid of being forced to undergo electro-shock! The former Chief Psychologist forced it on anyone who dared ever speak about what happens here."

"And that's a lot more scary than any monster." Elvira cleared her throat. "What Betty's trying to tell you is that, at our age, it's all too easy to be considered whacked—suffering from dementia—if what's said sounds too crazy."

The Sergeant looked perplexed. The Captain forced a wry smile. "We're only interested in whatever it is you've seen that chewed up those vehicles."

Elvira nodded. "I've come to call it Dreadful." She

looked toward the window. "It only does what it does because it's hungry." She tried to smile but only looked sad.

"Doesn't it frighten you?" the Captain asked.

"No," Elvira said. "It never comes as far as the buildings."

"Dreadful," the Captain said. "Why call it that?"

"What else would you call something so big it can swallow someone's car?"

"Gulp it down like a ham sandwich," Betty said. "And then spit it out again."

"It feeds off the vehicles?" the Captain frowned.

"And after what happened the first time anyone said anything... well, no resident ever dared to say a word ever again," Betty said. "Oh, Molly even tried to tell her priest, but he got indignant and told her not to talk like that or people would think she was crazy, maybe lock her up."

"And you think that's where it lives?" the Sergeant peered out at a knoll half-hidden by overgrown shrubbery.

"That was here before they built these apartments." Elvira said. "I believe there is some kind of old sewer system under that little hill. We don't know how long it's been there, though." She looked at Betty.

The Captain turned and gazed around the apartment. There were lacy curtains and patchwork cushions. The few books on a shelf were romance novels. He was sure, were these women given a polygraph, what they said would register as true.

"Because it would spit them out, we figured it was after the cars to drink the oil. And we discovered that if we put fresh motor oil out for it at the edge of the weedy part, it wouldn't come out at night and chew up the cars."

The Captain's eyes widened. "You put out motor oil for it?"

Betty nodded. "When we can afford to pick up a couple of cans."

"We walk down the hill to the gas station together." Elvira said. "Then at night we bring it out to it."

"What do you do?" asked the Sergeant.

Betty smiled. "I pour it into my dish pan and we leave it out there. Next day my pan is empty."

"I wonder if Dreadful's got any kin?" the Sergeant scratched his head. "I've heard tales from other states even, about cars and strange disappearances."

"Best to have the Governor request Special Forces," the Captain said. He took out his cell phone and punched in the Chief's number.

"Report!" The brisk voice crackled amidst static.

The Captain summarized what he had learned from the women. "Sir, it may sound far-fetched, but some form of toxic waste maybe, in the sewers under and around these buildings, has spawned a monster."

"That's preposterous!"

"Yes, sir," he said. "Apparently consumption of motor oil seems to satisfy its needs and keeps it calm. The residents here feed it."

He shook his head, frowned and handed the phone to the Sergeant.

"Best way I can put it, sir," the Sergeant said, "is that we're dealing with some sort of Creature From the

Black Lagoon living out behind the parking lot."

The familiar voice crackled amidst even more static. "Return to base immediately."

At the foot of the hill, an anonymous-looking blue panel truck was parked next to the pizza joint. Inside it, the News Editor from *Moment-to-Moment TV News* and four technicians sat amidst computers and digital recording devices. "We got it all down, boss," one technician said.

The News Editor waved his bottle of water. "Here's to 21st century news-gathering, and the perfection of satellite-guided encoded listening devices."

"We can hack it!" Several technicians sang out.

"And here's to the Dreadful," he grinned. "May it soon join Big Foot and the Loch Ness Monster in the Urban Legends Hall of Fame."

The Head Honcho at *Moment-to-Moment TV News* was not a happy man. He resented being chewed out by some faceless bureaucrat at the FCC for having broken the Dreadful story. Worse was their insistence that a retraction be released immediately stating that what had been reported was but a hoax perpetrated by college students.

"No need to cause panic in the streets," the bureaucrat said. "With all that's going on, there's no place in today's news for monsters!"

When he heard that the Feds had squashed the story, the News Editor sulked. "It never happened," he told his crew of skilled hackers. "The Dreadful story is officially dead."

"But now we know how to hack our way into anything," a technician boasted.

That morning, a convoy of military vehicles rolled into the senior housing complex. Thirty soldiers in battle dress emerged alongside technicians in white coats. Betty watched the soldiers cordon off the parking lot while the technicians walked around consulting complex instruments.

Sprawled in the perpetual darkness of its oil-soaked lair in the sewer pipes, Dreadful sensed unfamiliar energies and vibrations outside. Moving slowly through the pipes, it began to uncoil its twenty yards of black sludge.

The State Police Captain and Sergeant met with the men in charge of Operation Dreadful.

"We're not really here," one said. "Our unit doesn't exist."

The Sergeant pointed at the knoll. "Don't let your men get too close to that clearing, or they might disappear."

The Colonel pointed. "What's down that manhole anyway?"

"The Creature from the Black Lagoon, sir. Sustains itself on motor oil from vehicles small enough to swallow."

A technician waved his sensor. The dials twirled and lights flashed. "I'm picking up lots of flammable sludge, plus oil."

A small, balding man in a white lab coat joined the technicians. He studied their instrument panel and nodded. "Our gizmo's smart enough to do the job."

"You sending in a drone?" the Captain asked.

The Colonel shook his head. "That's classified. Within seconds, whatever's down there disintegrates. But like I said, we're not even here and none of this is even going on."

"Safer that way," the Captain nodded.

"Exactly," the officer said.

Elvira joined Betty at the window. "I hope they don't kill it," she said.

"Of course they'll kill it," Betty said. "While I was folding my laundry I heard someone say they'll blow it back to the Old Stone Age."

"But that is so unfair," Elvira said. "Besides, it has scientific value."

"Why?" Betty said.

"Because it's a monster that lives on motor oil. Think what science can learn by studying it."

Betty shook her head. "Even so, they're of the mind to exterminate it."

"Then they're being very foolish," Elvira huffed.

Betty sighed sympathetically. "It's not like there's anything we can do."

Elvira went to put on her shoes. "I'm going outside and tell whoever's in charge exactly what I think."

"I suppose," Betty said.

As they started across the parking lot the Chief Psychologist caught up with them. "And how are you ladies today?"

"We're here to talk sense into those people," Elvira said.

"Really," Betty said. "Otherwise they're going to blow it up."

"Yes," he said. His voice softened. "And did you two have a blow-up today?"

Elvira looked him in the eye. "We tried warning everybody about this."

"And for that we all owe you a vote of thanks." His voice took on a far-away tone.

"They need to know that they should take it alive so science can study it."

He gazed at them. "Whatever made you think they'd be foolish enough to do something like that?"

"Well, I heard someone say they were sending it back to the Old Stone Age." Betty said.

"Yes," his eyes lit up. He smiled. "So we have nothing to worry about now, do we?"

"Of course we do!" Elvira's voice rose.

"But don't you see, if something's blown back to The Old Stone Age, why that's completely different then blowing it into smithereens right here. That would cause damage."

"I don't see any difference." Elvira sounded indignant. "Don't you understand it lives on oil?"

"Back to the Old Stone Age," he smiled, not hearing what she was trying to tell him. Then he paused. "But yes, of course, you're absolutely right. Your thinking is really right on." He gave them the friendliest smile either had seen in a long time. He looked at them compassionately. "You must understand that these people are highly trained and know exactly what to do."

Elvira sighed. "If they're that smart, why not just put it to sleep, send it to a zoo, and study it?"

"They don't want monsters in zoos!" he shouted,

momentarily losing his cool. He stopped and collected himself. "Think how that would affect the other animals. Now ladies, really, it would be much better if you two went back to your nice apartment and watched one of your favorite TV programs. Let the government take care of monsters the way they know best."

Elvira persevered. "I just hope we're not all sent back into the Old Stone Age with it."

"I wouldn't let something like that bother you." He smiled. "We've got a pretty smart government. They would never let anything like that ever happen."

Elvira and Betty spent the rest of the day in their apartment. Betty sat on the couch and knitted. Elvira read a little and fidgeted. "I wasn't afraid of monsters when I was a kid," she said. "I really felt sad for days after seeing that horrid ending to *King Kong*." She grimaced. "Kong deserved better."

Betty nodded. "That movie made me cry. I'm going to make some macaroni and cheese for supper. Want some?"

"Sure. That Chief Psychologist really upsets me. Him thinking he's the cat's meow that way. Why, to him we're just two daft old ladies. Well, someday he'll get his."

"I wish you wouldn't think of us that way," Betty said. "Just remember, it's easy to keep feeling young even if most others think we're over the hill." She opened the fridge and popped a can of cream soda.

"You drinking that rat poison again?" Elvira said.

"At my age, who cares? It tastes good."

"Sure," Elvira said. "No one ever said we're supposed to be smart and make sense."

Betty looked at Elvira and shrugged. "I never tried to make sense. At least not the sense other people expected me to make. I do think I made my own sense most of the time; and those times I don't, well, we can't always be perfect."

Elvira sighed. "Times like this I wish I had a cigarette."

"That's why I like cream soda. It keeps me young."

"What's that supposed to mean?"

Betty smiled. "That if some handsome octogenarian at the senior center offered me a cream soda I might let myself get a little carried away."

It was getting dark. Elvira walked to the window. Soldiers had unrolled a thick blue tarp that blanketed the parking lot. "You really think they'll keep Dreadful a secret?"

"Of course they will." Betty said. "Look at how they deny anything about flying saucers. Monsters fall into a similar category."

Tears filled Elvira's eyes. A large refrigeration vehicle drove onto the tarp. "Look!" Elvira pointed. "That's like something out of a science fiction movie." She covered her eyes. "They're going to execute it." Then she smiled. "But maybe Dreadful can't be destroyed. We don't really know."

"I wonder how many others like it there might be?" Betty said. "It's frightening to imagine them crawling in sewers all over the country."

"Don't go there," Elvira said.

Betty smirked. "Trying to make sense out of all this

is like trying to control the wind."

Elvira smiled. "Maybe he'll invite you to the Cape."

"Who?"

"The octogenarian at the senior center who'll offer you the cream soda." She forced a smile. "Assuming you'd really want to flirt with him."

Betty's eyes widened. "Oh, that would be nice. Yes, I'd like that. Come away from the window, Elvira. You just can't take this so personally. Nothing personal to Dreadful, but it's just how they act around monsters. Very defensive." She took a box of macaroni and cheese from the cupboard and made it. They shared supper, watched a little TV, and went to bed.

Around three in the morning, a series of piercing, high-frequency sounds awoke Elvira. It could have been a large flock of birds, but not in the middle of the night. Betty was asleep. Elvira got out of bed and went to the window. She leaned out and looked. The refrigeration vehicle was positioned near the shrubbery. Long steel tubes extended from it and pointed downward into the manhole opening. The vehicle shook and shuddered. The air around it was steamy. Elvira sighed and shook her head. "Poor Dreadful! What are they doing to you?"

The following morning the soldiers were gone. The parking lot looked just as it always had. In their bathrobes and slippers, Betty and Elvira went outside and walked toward the knoll. To Elvira the air felt cold with an icy hint to it. It seemed like slithers of winter had been wedged between the warm breezes of summer.

Elvira sighed. "I feel so sad about Dreadful."

Betty put her arm around her friend's shoulders.

"You did all you could to save it, but some things are out of our hands."

Elvira sniffed the air. "What on earth could that smell possibly be?" She thought a minute, "It's a little like the kind of chemical they put into air conditioners." Betty laughed. "Maybe they froze it to death or something. Let's go make breakfast."

They turned and walked back to their apartment. "I haven't even washed my face." Elvira said.

Betty started the coffeemaker and put two English muffins in the toaster oven. Elvira went into the bathroom. There in the sink by the drain wriggled a little black speck. Elvira watched as it slithered across the white porcelain.

"Dreadful!" she reached down and carefully scooped it into the palm of her hand. "Dreadful! Some of you is still alive." She rushed into the kitchen to show Betty.

"Oh my!" Betty said.

"Let's give it a little jar and some cooking oil for now. Later on we can get some high octane stuff at the gas station." From a drawer she took an eyedropper and gently fed some oil to the little swigging speck. "We'll keep you here until you get bigger," she said, "and then we'll let you go."

The End—Maybe

The Scrapbook

Since the death of his wife, Irv had made the best of being alone. The corner deli was steps away—although he seemed to be losing his appetite. His bank, a pharmacy, and the library were nearby. He would say he didn't have a care in the world. Well, he thought that might be an exaggeration. He rubbed his hand through his thinning white hair. A short, lean man with bright blue eyes, he still, in his mid-eighties, enjoyed a game of ping-pong. Though lately he had to admit he'd slowed down a lot.

Now he cut away the tape and opened the just delivered package. Unfolding the wrapping, he picked up the legal looking paper that was on top of the old fashioned scrapbook. A spasm shook his chest and he coughed. He took a sip of water and peered at the writing. It seemed he was the beneficiary of his Aunt Rose's legendary scrapbook. He'd heard about it in his boyhood, but had forgotten about it. He was the last of his family—probably why the scrapbook came to him, he thought.

Aunt Rose was renowned as the family historian. She had dedicated herself to keeping track of every cousin and relative, however distant. Here was the history of his entire family laid out before him. He turned the pages slowly. Although they were unknown to him, the faces on sepia cabinet cards in the opening pages were somehow familiar. Others in later, candid snapshots sparked the same kind of feeling.

How can you feel so close to those you've never seen or heard of before? He wondered as he looked at the faces in newspaper clippings of weddings and births. Aunt Rose had captured the essence of his family. He looked at the clock and sighed. He shivered. Time to take his pills. He wished they did something to help alleviate the ache in his legs. His heart would skip a beat now and then but he knew he didn't want doctors messing with him.

He swallowed a handful of the over-the-counter meds from the pharmacy. They seemed to do the trick, pretty much, though not as much as they used to. Feeling excited for the first time in a while, he wrapped a scarf around his neck and went back to the scrapbook. Once again he gazed at the faded sepia portraits of unknown, 19th-century European faces. How remarkably familiar they were. He noticed that each relative had his or her own page. Their names were carefully hand-lettered by Aunt Rose's meticulous yet old-fashioned handwriting. He felt a sense of deep wonder, knowing all of their lives were laid out before him.

During his boyhood his favorite was Aunt Blanch, his father's younger sister. She had died from cancer shortly after his nineteenth birthday. He found her page and was taken by her loving smile. She had encouraged him. Insisted he go to college. Told him he was handsome despite what he considered an over-sized nose and ears.

Tears sprang to his eyes. There she was as a teenager wearing a ballet skirt. He hadn't known she danced. Then he remembered his father saying she had damaged a leg skating shortly after high school. He rubbed his eyes. Did she just wink at him or was that his imagination? Tears dampened his face, tears from an unexplainable sense of joy. Even now he could feel her love.

He went to his Uncle Abe's page. He looked so poised in his World War One officer's uniform. Irv knew Abe served on General Pershing's staff and had been awarded several medals. Gazing at Aunt Rose's photos, Irv felt the man's pride and dedication. He also felt his approval, something he did not remember from his youth.

He paused and looked up at the clock. Almost time for supper. He looked back at the scrapbook. Aunt Rose had achieved something special. She had captured each relative's essence, creating a kind of immortality. His parents' wedding photograph was on his father's page, along with a carefully printed listing of his awards and achievements. His mom looked happy that day. Something rare for him to see and he was glad for it. They seemed so alive.

Night was coming. Irv set the scrapbook aside and put on his warm sweater. Though he had many, this was the only one he'd wear. Marion had given it to him that last birthday they were together. Wearing it brought her closer to him. He started coughing. What ever had made him start smoking? His father had smoked and passed sooner than he had to. He coughed and pressed the inhalant between his teeth. He began feeling heartburn. But he could breathe again. He continued to turn the pages. Through the window the sun was just about down and he could see the twilight sky.

The light seemed to flicker. The room grew dark. Turning to the last page of the scrapbook he saw his own name carefully hand lettered by Aunt Rose. His eyes widened. Beneath it appeared a heading for his obituary. The daylight was fading. He could see a light somewhere in the distance. A slight breeze blew over the scrapbook, rippling the pages. The friendly faces smiled up at him. He closed the scrapbook, stood up, and went toward the light.

A Helping Hand

It was Christmas Eve and Ned and Jenny were "nestled all snug in their beds." Or at least they were supposed to be. Their mom and dad sat downstairs wrapping a few last minute gifts. Their budget was tight this year. The pile of presents was smaller than usual. "Company's coming for dinner. Tomorrow will be a long day." Dad yawned, turned off the lights and followed Mom upstairs to bed.

Ned was seven, daring, and extremely curious. He climbed out of bed and pulled his jeans and Spider Man sweatshirt on over his pajamas. Then he added his padded down vest and slippers.

Jenny was five. She yawned and rubbed her eyes, got up, and put her puffy vest over her robe and pajamas. Jenny staunchly maintained that anything her brother could do, she could do too.

Ned pressed his fingers to his lips. "Talk softly. Mustn't wake them up or we'll be in trouble."

"For sure, we'll have a better chance to see the reindeer land Santa's sleigh on the roof if we wait by the attic window," Jenny said.

Jenny tiptoed behind her brother into the second floor hallway and then up the attic stairs. A dull thud sounded near the chimney.

Startled, Ned pulled open the attic door, crossed the wide floor and peered toward the window. "What was that?" He ran over and pushed the window open. Jenny crowded in next to him and looked out. Though they could hear movement they couldn't see anyone, especially not a jolly old man with a long white beard in a red suit and black boots.

Ned leaned out. "Over here," he called out. "Come in through here." But no one responded. It was windy. Maybe he wasn't heard. He clutched his flashlight and thought about climbing out of the window onto the sloped roof. He'd done it a lot during daylight, but hadn't when it was cold, dark, and windy with flurries of snow blustering against the house.

"Are we going out there?" Jenny asked.

The snow slapped against the window.

"Are you there?" Ned called out. He craned his neck and pushed himself farther out. "You must be! Me and my sister heard your sled when you landed."

"Maybe it was just the wind," Jenny said. She was feeling doubtful, not to mention cold. "Maybe," she said, "this isn't such a good idea."

But Ned ignored her. Leaning even farther out the window he said, "We've cookies for you on the table next to the Christmas tree. Wouldn't it be easier for you to come in and go through the house instead of down the chimney?"

There was no response. Yet it seemed they could hear someone moving around. All they could see was windy clumps of swirling snow.

"You stay here," Ned told his sister with all the authority a seven year old could muster.

"No way," Jenny said. "If you go out there, I'm

going too."

"But what if something happens? What if you fall off? Then I'll be in trouble big-time. No, you stay inside."

"Forget it," Jenny said. She giggled, thinking she sounded like Mom when she was determined to do something her way.

Ned pushed himself up onto the sill and stepped out the window. The wind blew it shut before Jenny could follow after him.

"Oh!" His feet began slipping out from under him. He panicked and dropped his flashlight. His feet flew out and he started sliding toward the edge.

"Oh, help Help!" he cried. As he gazed up at the swirling snow he saw a pair of dark boots. Then a gloved hand grabbed the back of his vest and he stopped falling.

His teeth chattered. He shivered and shook. Without a word, whoever held onto him pushed opened the attic window and lifted him back inside. The window slammed shut. Tears rolled down Jenny's white face. She clutched Ned's cold hands.

"Did you see him?" He huddled inside his down vest.

"See who?" Jenny asked.

"See who kept me from falling off the roof and opened the window and lifted me back inside! Was it Santa Claus? Didn't you see?"

"I didn't see anyone except you coming back in."

"But someone grabbed a hold of me before I got blown off the roof. It had to be him. Who else would be outside on our roof late at night on Christmas Eve?"

"Don't tell Mom anything about this," Jenny said, "or she'll get really upset. It's too cold up here. I want to go back downstairs."

Ned frowned. "Girls! If you'd gone out there and someone picked you up and put you back inside the window I'd sure know who it was."

Jenny didn't reply. She turned and went back down the attic stairs. Ned followed her. They climbed into their beds and went back to sleep.

The following morning the children awoke before their parents. Excited, they quickly dressed and hurried downstairs. Neither mentioned what happened last night in the attic.

Under the tree they found presents wrapped in colorful Christmas paper. Set to one side was a pair of special boots and a mountain climbing kit. The large tag read, "for Ned." The cookies on the table by the side of the Christmas tree were gone. In their place was his flashlight.

The Telephone

Karen and Pete loved the old Cape. The price was right and they jumped at it. Pete loved the stone fireplace, hearth, and wide pine floorboards. Karen fell in love with the slope of the roof, the original fluted glass window panes, and especially the antique crank telephone built into the wall of the kitchen. She lifted the receiver, heard only silence, laughed and hung up.

"Just for looks," she said. "Unless you want to install a land line in it."

But Pete shook his head. "We couldn't do that. Historic relics must be preserved. It's a part of the house. Besides we've got our cell phones."

During the next two weeks the Cape was totally refurbished and brought into the 21st century. They moved in a month later. Though married for close to five years, living in the Cape made them feel like newlyweds.

"Ours," Pete said feeling manly and responsible. He wandered from room to room.

"Ours," Karen agreed knowing that here was where she would raise her family.

Just then the phone in the kitchen rang.

It was a different sort of ring, more the sound of a bicycle bell than a phone. She was making pancakes. What kind of a joke is this? She thought, picking it up.

The silence gave way to garbled sounds. Karen held

the earpiece away from her and stared at it. Then an elderly female voice said. "Karen? Is that you? This is Aunt Mae."

Karen's stomach lurched, her face reddened and she almost dropped the receiver.

"But you're gone, Aunt Mae. For a long time now." Her voice sounded shaky and small.

"What are you saying dear?"

"That you're dead," she sputtered. Tears filled her eyes.

"Of course not," Aunt Mae said. "Women who cook never die. We just go to a bigger kitchen."

The line went dead.

She hung it up and rushed into the den. Pete was at his computer contemplating e-trades on the net.

She told him.

He stood up, hugged her and gently stroked her head. "Sounds like there's more stress in moving than either of us realized."

"I'm not stressed," she said firmly.

"Of course not." He stroked her hair. "Maybe your imagination got the better of you. You know, one of those waking dreams."

"I wasn't dreaming!" Her voice rose. Then she clamped her lips, turned, and opened the fridge.

They had supper, or he did. She had lost her appetite and decided to turn in early.

Pete kissed her. "I'll clean up in here," he smiled. "Oh, what a wonderful home we have!" Then he kissed her again and she climbed the stairs to bed.

Several minutes later the bicycle bell ring sounded.

Pete frowned, looked at the phone and reluctantly picked up the receiver.

"Pete? That you?"

He gulped. "Uncle Joe? It's you?"

He heard a familiar laugh. Then the smell of his uncle's cigar filled the kitchen. "I've only a moment. Tomorrow before noon pick up twenty five thousand shares of Amalgamated Concrete. You can afford it! You've got that much in savings."

Pete wondered what was going on. He knew the stock. It was a loser.

"I don't think so, Uncle Joe." His hands trembled. Was he speaking with a ghost? His uncle had been dead for... he'd lost count of the years.

"Listen to me," Joe said sternly. "You make that buy tomorrow before noontime. Don't disappoint me." The line went dead.

Pete felt dizzy. His body began to shake; his teeth chattered. He poured himself a drink. Then he went to his computer and looked up Amalgamated Concrete. The stock listed for a dollar a share.

Karen was sleeping when he came in. Still shivering, he climbed out of his clothes and into bed beside her. This was just too strange.

The following morning Pete told several of his co-workers about his stock tip. They laughed. Despite this and feeling like a fool, at eleven thirty he emptied their savings account and bought twenty five thousand shares of Amalgamated.

The acquisition was announced at noon. A Saudi Prince thought Amalgamated was the way to go. The stock split at sixty to one.

Pete called Karen and shared the good news. "Make a reservation at your favorite restaurant," he said. He left work early, bounced into the cabin and swept his wife up in his arms. Then he presented her with a bouquet of American Beauty roses. "What's up?" he asked. "You're not smiling."

She hugged him and started to cry. "I think I'm losing my mind. That phone rang again. It was Aunt Mae. She said now that we're rich it was a good idea to put on a deck."

"Maybe after we get back from that vacation you've always wanted," Pete said. "Now let's go have dinner."

From time to time, at special occasions like the birth of their first child, the old telephone would ring and a familiar family voice would share something helpful. Pete and Karen cherished these moments and grew to look forward to their rare occurrence. One day, after several children, they realized they had outgrown the Cape and with their burgeoning family, reluctantly moved to a bigger, more spacious home.

They had to leave the old telephone behind. Karen often wondered if it ever rang for the newly married couple that bought their old Cape.

The Gift

Once upon a time, in a serene country town, there lived a bright seven-year-old boy named Kevin who had absolutely everything any child could ever possibly want. His room was filled with all the best toys, books, games, DVDs, and electronic gadgets conceivable. As anyone might imagine, Christmas shopping was an extremely difficult task for his parents.

"How about one of those new iPods that can hold a thousand hours worth of music?" Grandfather asked.

"Too late," his father said ruefully. "We already gave him one."

"A new digital movie camera perhaps?" Kindly Grandmother suggested.

But his mother shook her head. "No, we bought him one for his birthday," she lamented.

"A pony might be perfect," Uncle Chuck put in between swallows of holiday grog. Uncle Chuck was known amongst the family for his tremendous agility at spending other people's money at a record pace.

"No," the father shook his head. "He doesn't like horses. Besides, I think there are town ordinances we'd have to take into consideration."

"What do you give a child who has everything?" Kindly Grandmother asked wistfully.

"Maybe a big treasure chest to keep it all in," Grandfather chuckled. "Then he could play with everything we've given him one at a time instead of all at once."

"Just look at our predicament! If we hadn't already given him everything under the sun, we wouldn't be all fussed wondering what to give him now," Kindly Grandmother sighed.

Kevin came into the room. "Tell us," they begged. "What would you like for Christmas?"

The boy turned and looked out the window at the speck of moon far off in the distant sky. "I don't know," he said wistfully. Then he smiled and his eyes brightened as he pointed toward the window. "Give me the moon," he said resolutely. "Yes! I want the moon for Christmas."

"Whatever for?" his mother asked, a touch of mild indignation in her usually serene voice.

"Then I can say it's mine," he replied. "And once it's mine, once it's really mine, then when I grow up I can become the man in the moon."

"But what would you do with the moon?" Grandfather asked shrewdly.

The child smiled. "I'm not sure," he said, sounding eminently logical. "Besides, it isn't mine yet. But once it is then I'll know and be able to tell you."

"Pricey piece of real estate," Uncle Chuck laughed. "You could always open a hotel for space travelers."

Kevin nodded and looked as seriously as possible at his family. Then he smiled. "That's what I really want for Christmas," he said gleefully while looking out at that distant speck so far away in the sky.

"We'll see," his father equivocated. "After all, big presents like that are really up to Saint Nick."

As the weeks passed and Christmas Day approached Kevin noticed that the Moon seemed larger and closer than when he first asked for it. "Santa's really bringing me the moon! It's so close!" he announced.

"Just a big ball of uninhabitable green cheese," Grandfather said, alluding to ancient lore.

"Who needs it anyway?" Kindly Grandmother followed suit. She realized that anyone who ever promised his or her child the moon was making a big mistake.

By Christmas Eve the moon was bright and full in the sky. Kevin was asleep dreaming of space ships and moonwalks. "Are you prepared to take full charge of this satellite?" a stern voice suddenly awoke him. "Do all the maintenance required for keeping a world-class planetary satellite in first-class shape?"

Kevin opened his eyes. He saw none other than Santa Claus standing at the foot of his bed. He looked a lot like he did in pictures only perhaps a little tired and definitely more cranky and impatient than he imagined.

"I have to make sure, before turning the deed to the Moon over to you, that you fully understand the responsibilities and commitments involved." He sounded more like a stern adult than some jolly old being that delivered gifts every year.

"You know, of course, there's lots of work involved with running the moon. But if you're willing to wake up every morning while it's still dark and not finish until minutes before supper, everyday, rain or shine, then I'll gladly turn these documents over to you." He waved official looking papers in Kevin's direction. "Personally, I think a bag of marbles would be lots more fun. Take a moment or two and think it over, then tell me your

decision. But hurry, I haven't got all night." Santa
sounded very businesslike.

Kevin yawned and blinked his eyes several times. He
thought about how difficult a task it would be keeping
the Moon mowed and raked and polished and always
looking beautiful. "What you're saying doesn't sound
like any fun to me at all," he complained. Santa nodded
in agreement. "Could I just have a look at that bag of
marbles?" he asked.

On Christmas morning Kevin's grandparents,
parents, and even Uncle Chuck gathered about the
Christmas tree exchanging gifts. Surprisingly, Kevin
seemed to have forgotten all about the moon.
Neglecting to open any other gifts, he seemed quite
content with an oddly designed cloth bag filled with
beautiful, colorful, antique agate marbles no one could
remember having purchased.

Mr. Perkins' Wallet

Mr. Perkins tried to make it a point to carefully avoid the twinkle in a woman's eyes. That sort of body language made him nervous. He felt that regular eyes that looked straight ahead were sufficient and twinkles only complicated the issue.

It had been three years since Mrs. Perkins' passing. Until now no woman had winked or flirted or even tried to strike up a conversation with him.

Wearing a floral skirt and pretty red blouse, she was sitting at a table at the weekly Saturday craft fair at the Senior Center. When she noticed him she waved then beckoned him to join her. Even thought he'd never seen her before, his heart skipped a beat. She smiled and even threw him a kiss. He went over to her table.

"Do I know you?" he asked. "You look familiar but I believe we've never met." He unfolded a chair and sat down across from her and introduced himself.

"Not yet," she smiled. "But I couldn't help recognize you. You are so famous. I absolutely adore your poetry. It is so moving."

His words stumbled. "I'm really sorry, but I've never written a poem in my life. You must have me confused with someone else."

"But the soul of a poet lives within you." Her eyes twinkled. "Wouldn't you like to experience creativity and self expression?"

It was the Saturday of the first craft show at the Senior Center. He noticed people checking out the other tables. There was a buzz of conversation.

She put her hand over his. "May I ask you a very personal question?"

He nodded.

"When was the last time you treated yourself to a new wallet?"

He squinted and pursed his lips. "I'm not really sure. I'm perfectly happy with the one I have."

"But maybe if you had a new one you might start writing poetry."

He found her smile enticing. "If I were a younger man I'd buy all your wallets and give them to my friends. But, these days, I'm sure the wallet I have is perfectly sufficient."

"Piffle," she said. "Every man needs a new wallet to perk up his life."

"May I ask why?" He had never heard such a claim.

"A new wallet can be magical." She waved her hands over her wares, looked intent and lowered her voice. "These are magical wallets made by a true wizard. I kid you not."

"Well in that case," Mr. Perkins chuckled and smiled at her.

She pouted. "You don't believe a word I'm saying, do you?"

Not wanting to appear rude he smiled. "Frankly, no."

"In that case," she sounded determined, "I insist upon making a present of one to you. If it isn't the most marvelously magical wallet you've ever had you may return it to me next Saturday."

Mr. Perkins frowned. "I can't really turn down an offer like that, can I?"

Her hand reached over his, picked one out and gave it to him. "This dark leather one is perfect. It matches your eyes." The wallet felt very comfortable in his hand.

He thanked her. "What makes them magical?"

"You'll have to ask the wizard," she smiled.

He especially liked the softness of the leather. "Please accept this as a special gift from me to you. I'm Maga."

Other customers began to crowd around her table.

"Next Saturday." She smiled and patted his hand.

At a table in the snack bar he transferred his cards, cash, and everything else to his new wallet. Despite how much he put into it, it still folded flat.

Then at the counter he ordered a club sandwich and coffee. Without thinking he opened his new wallet and extracted what he thought were three one-dollar bills.

"Nothing smaller?" The volunteer asked handing him back two. "Those are hundreds!"

"They are?" His voice shook. His eyes widened.

"Right. Don't you have anything smaller?"

"But I thought I just handed you three ones. Or is this a bank error that fortunately I've snagged in time?"

"I'll run you a tab. Pay sometime next week."

Worried that his checking account was terribly overdrawn, after gulping down lunch he rushed to his car and made a beeline to the bank. The ATM line was long. He waited impatiently. Finally, when he checked the machine, he saw that his account balance was correct minus the forty dollars he'd withdrawn for the weekend.

He drove back to the senior center. The courtyard was empty. The merchants had all left. Here was a situation he had to ponder. Where did those hundred dollar bills come from?

Back home he eyed his new wallet suspiciously and prayed that the bills were genuine currency and not counterfeit. He hid them inside his top bureau drawer under his suspenders.

The next morning at church without thinking he reached into his new wallet expecting to extract his usual two ones. Instead he saw himself put two hundred dollar bills in the plate.

The usher raised his eyes and regarded Mr. Perkins with newfound admiration. "How wonderful if others in the congregation would give that way," he thought.

Mr. Perkins felt bewildered. He gasped for breath. His head spun. He surmised that the only way to explain this predicament was to realize that his new wallet was seriously defective.

After the service, Mr. Perkins approached his minister. "Could we have a word?"

"Henry Perkins! Good to see you. I've already heard about your generosity. And I want to thank you."

"But that's just it," Mr. Perkins said. "I wasn't being generous. I put in two ones but they came out two hundreds."

His minister nodded. He had known Henry Perkins for years. He had grieved alongside Henry at Helen's grave. He patted his parishioner's shoulder.

"Two ones! Ha, Ha! Henry, you're quite the joker. Just don't want anyone else to know, huh?" He nodded. "Your secret's safe with me."

"But... but you don't understand," he sputtered. "When I open my wallet expecting to take out a dollar, I get a hundred."

The minister gave him his best toothy grin. "Henry, your sense of giving is even beyond you," he laughed. "Maybe you're coming down with elephantiasis of the generosity?"

Then his voice took on newfound sagacity. "You know, Henry, back in Seminary, when the old Revs would come and talk to us, whenever they'd get around to the subject of church finances, they'd always tell us that cash is king and shrouds don't have pockets." He patted Henry on the shoulder.

Mr. Perkins nodded. He knew this conversation was hopeless.

Sadly, throughout the ensuing week, the guilt that arose when he'd try to accept this good luck became paranoia that Treasury agents were lying in wait for him, ready to slam him into jail for passing counterfeit hundred dollar bills.

After a hurried breakfast on Saturday he rushed over to the Senior Center determined to get some real answers from this Mata Hari who sold defective wallets.

"Good morning." He stood at her table.

"Well hello," she looked up and smiled. "You came back. I had hoped you would." Her eyes twinkled for all to see.

"Whenever I take out a dollar what comes out is a hundred. It's very unnerving."

"Oh, you poor dear!" She smiled and patted his hand. "Yes. I imagine it must be. I'm so terribly sorry for this inconvenience, but I fear Old Zeke's been at it again."

"Old Zeke? Who's Old Zeke?"

"Old Zeke's the wizard in Phoenix who makes the wallets."

"No one else has complained?"

"You're the first I know to call attention to it."

She swept her hands across the other wallets perhaps assuring them.

"I'll certainly make good on my offer. Just pick out another."

"If you don't mind my asking," Mr. Perkins said, "how exactly does he do that?"

"Search me. Best I can tell you is that sometimes before he sews them he'll hex the leather with what he calls his 'Abracadabra Moonshine'."

"What exactly do you mean?"

She shrugged her shoulders. "You'll have to ask Old Zeke."

"I see." Mr. Perkins wondered if she and this Zeke character were a part of a counterfeit ring.

"But I can remove that particular hex. If you'd like I'll do it right now. She took his wallet from him, reached in her bag, and pulled out a polished wooden wand. She closed her eyes, murmured some words he couldn't hear, and waved the wand over his wallet. She breathed deeply. Her face reddened. After what seemed an eternity she clapped her hands and opened her eyes.

"That should do it. But if you'd rather have another…"

"No, no, not as long as you fixed it." He smiled. "I do like how it feels in my pocket."

She patted his hand. "I can't guarantee that my hex removal remedy works every time."

"Just so long as there are no more hundred dollar bills." Mr. Perkins was emphatic. "After all, enough is enough."

"That I can assure you. There won't be any more of those, I promise."

"Well, in that case," He put his new wallet back in his pocket, rose, thanked her for her generosity, then left the Senior Center and drove to the market to pick up a few things he needed for the weekend.

At checkout he opened his new wallet expecting to extract two tens. Instead Confederate bank notes flew out onto the counter. The faces of Stonewall Jackson and Jefferson Davis glared hard at him.

The clerk's eyes widened. He appeared confused. "You can't pay with that kind of money anymore, I don't think."

Mr. Perkins felt baffled. He gulped and prayed no one had noticed what had just transpired.

"Wait a minute. Here's my credit card." But before he could remove it a flurry of scowling Robert E Lee banknotes flew out. He slapped it shut before other rebels could escape, swept the pile of Confederate bills into the bag with his orange juice, frozen pizza and cans of soda. "Just old money," he mumbled handing the clerk his card.

When he got home he separated the confederate currency from his groceries, then he took his new wallet from his pocket. Removing the papers and cards and cash, he looked at it, frowned and shook his head. He sensed a sadness he couldn't explain. Going upstairs to his bedroom he opened his top bureau drawer and retrieved his old wallet. Then with a sigh, he looked at his new one and regretfully hid it at the back of the drawer under his handkerchiefs.

A Matter of Great Importance

George firmly believed that achieving absolute importance was the key to a successful life. To George, feeling important was equal to pitching a no-hitter or scoring the winning touchdown in the Super Bowl. Not only did importance reflect, in his estimation, the only true measure of one's life work, but without it the planet, he felt, was doomed.

Each night as he lay in bed, half of him was back at work in his Dilbert-style cubical tallying endless streams of numbers. He believed that, to achieve sufficient importance, one must know how to work in one's sleep. And then one night he had a dream of attaining great wealth and fame. He awoke feeling incredibly important.

After work the next day he gathered several of his closest associates at a restaurant, where he proposed a plan that could ultimately result in not only far greater importance for each of them, but also wealth beyond their imagining.

Nodding in agreement, Alfred an attorney said, "There must be millions of others just like us who feel the exact same way we do. I'll draw up the title and get started on incorporation."

"No reason why we can't help ourselves attain wealth through importance." Jim, a marketing pro, grinned mischievously and rubbed his hands.

"Best not to waste any more time," William, a time management expert, insisted. "We must begin immediately or someone else will run the ball."

Moments later, on George's yellow legal pad, the Universal Brotherhood of Absolute Importance was born.

Jim proposed that, to begin with, charter members of UBAI receive a mahogany plaque with a gold nameplate and a quarterly newsletter stressing the value of importance throughout everyday life.

That night home in bed, as the founder of the enviable Universal Brotherhood of Absolute Importance, George began to feel his own self-esteem expand. During the weeks and months ahead, just as they had anticipated and despite its exorbitant initiatory fees, thousands of membership applications were received and processed. Quickly, however, George and his associates realized that a commodity of even greater value than mere importance was exclusivity.

Jim suggested that the members' annual meeting not be held in the USA. Instead he showed a brochure for an exclusive five star hotel located somewhere in the tropics near the rain forest. There, members might flex their importance amidst natural foliage at rates far below those charged at traditional conference centers.

"We need a headliner, a guest speaker of inordinate importance," Alfred urged. "Someone who will make the rest of us sit up and take notice without, of course, threatening our self-importance one bit."

George, Jim, and William readily agreed that such a keynote speaker was essential to the ultimate success of the first Annual Meeting. They sat in their new posh office and deliberated who this headliner might be.

True to his profession, Alfred argued for a Supreme Court Justice, someone of vital importance who could lay down the law in a bipartisan and entertaining fashion.

William wanted a Fortune 500 CEO, whose name would immediately enhance everyone's sense of self-importance.

Jim pushed for something more show-biz: an Oscar winner, a batting champ, or a Super Bowl MVP. By hobnobbing with an all star, he insisted, those in attendance would feel more important than even their membership plaque and special quarterly newsletter could signify.

It was George who suggested The Swami. Excitedly he handed his partners photographs of a small, seemingly insignificant bearded man clad only in a loincloth and turban. While his demeanor was demure his press was astounding. It included eyewitness accounts of his being able to fly and to appear in more than one locale at the same time.

George assured the others that they would be doing the right thing having The Swami as their first headliner. What sealed the deal was a *Daily News* photo article. It showed his disciples in Northern India celebrating The Swami's birthday each year by bestowing upon him his weight in diamonds and rare gems.

"The only swami ever to be paid to endorse a Rolex," George said with intense admiration. That alone seemed sufficient to his partners. An invitation was sent to The Swami inviting him to headline this most auspicious first Annual Meeting.

Days later The Swami not only agreed to participate in this storied event but, furthermore, suggested that the

meeting and all festivities be held in his mountainside
village of Shangri La-La, specifically in his mystical
palace of earthly delights, lost within the clouds that
hover around Mt. Everest. Here, he assured George and
the other principals of UBAI, the entire membership
could best taste the riches of prosperity and self-
adulation as well as experience the primal pleasures of
the senses.

George, Jim, William and Alfred were thrilled. They
felt totally relieved. All the work was being done for
them. All they had to do was pack their bags and depart
at the designated time. The Swami's staff apparently
would take care of every minute detail. Would-be
attendees were notified to gather in the parking lot of
the UBAI offices where they would depart for the
conference.

Several months later, eight hundred men and women
of self-realized prominence stood with their baggage at
the entrance of the UBIA parking lot, eagerly awaiting
and anticipating their journey to Shangri La-La.

Nervously, George joined the others in the parking
lot as they waited to leave for their First Annual
Conference on Importance in Shangri La-La.

"Where are the buses?" William asked. "They're
late!" He consulted his watch and made a mental note to
put punctuality at the top of the agenda for the next
board meeting of the Universal Brotherhood of
Absolute Importance.

Other participants arrived, parked, and waited beside
their baggage. Some chatted quietly, others leafed

through *Importance,* the Society's newsletter.

Suddenly, The Swami appeared. He bowed graciously and waved his right hand several times. The parking lot swirled with mist. When it cleared, all gazed upon a towering castle, presumably in the snow-covered mountains of Shangri La-La.

They looked at one another in amazement. Their business suits had been transformed into brightly-colored, jewel-embroidered silken garments worthy of a Maharaja.

The Swami beckoned them into the castle and led them to a magnificent banquet hall. As they sat down in throne-like golden chairs, he bowed before them. "To attain the realization of unlimited importance is why we are here." Cheers and shouts of agreement filled the great hall.

"To attain unlimited importance, you must first attain unlimited unimportance." Confused faces greeted him. "True insignificance, absolute indifference, genuine unimportance," he went on.

A murmur arose.

"This Hindu stuff is deep," Alfred mumbled. He was curious whether the gems sewn into his robes were real.

"But isn't one's true importance determined by his station, accomplishments, and circumstances attained throughout a lifetime?" Jim asked.

The Swami looked intently into Jim's eyes. "The ant is of unlimited importance, as is the honey bee, as well as the elephant. All creatures attain a sense of natural recognition within their unimportance." The Swami closed his eyes and lifted his head. "Without ant, bee or elephant, the planet faces upheaval. Be the elephant, be the bee, be the ant; let the true essence of your being emerge."

This guidance was clearly lost on Alfred. "How can I be an elephant? I'm not a Republican!"

Jim was perplexed, William confused. George wondered what The Swami was talking about.

The Swami smiled and gently waved his hand. Alfred felt his body stretch and elongate; gigantic tusks sprouted from either side of his whiskers. His voice became a loud high-pitched screech. Suddenly all the participants became elephants. Their trumpeting was deafening. Then in the blinking of an eye they buzzed like bees around hives filled with honey. Then they lost their wings and fell to the ground as tiny ants.

As they milled about in confusion, they found themselves once again seated in their golden throne-like chairs. The Swami smiled. "See yourselves throughout your many incarnations," he said, "each one important, or unimportant as the case may be, depending upon you and your point of view."

The participants shook their heads. "What's all this about?" William inquired. George looked dazed. The Swami raised his hands. In the absolute silence that followed, a flute melody encircled the room. Each participant felt everything about himself or herself fall away except the knowledge of who they really were.

"See the purity and innocence that is your essence as the immortal child travels throughout eons of time and Light." The Swami smiled, gestured, and an immediate burst of brilliant sunlight filled the great hall. "Children," he said. "You are children of the Eternal Light."

The Swami beckoned and maidens in colorful silk

saris, carrying ewers of wine, stopped before each participant and filled their silver goblets. Then a sumptuous banquet was laid out before them. "Feast here, and know that your true essence now emerges from behind those walls of fear and doubt you create for your own protection."

A lovely maiden stopped before George. She bowed and looked into his eyes. For a moment he felt in the depths of his being his true immortal nature. She nodded in recognition and placed a thin gold ring on the little finger of his left hand. Smiling, she touched the side of his cheek and moved on. Tears sprang to his eyes. Blinking, he gazed about him. Others were having a like experience. He saw The Swami suspended above them, enveloped in a glow of golden light that radiated throughout the great hall. He took a deep breath and closed his eyes. He felt completely satisfied. Nothing was important any more.

When next he opened his eyes he found himself back in the parking lot along with the rest of the participants. He saw a newspaper lying on the ground. It was dated Sunday. But hadn't they just left? "Three days have passed?" he said. "How can that be?"

No one said very much. People got into their cars and left. George noticed the small gold ring on the little finger of his left hand. William, Jim, and Alfred each had one too. "When should we have another UBAI meeting?" he asked.

"I dunno," said Alfred.

"What for?" asked William.

"Maybe meetings aren't all that important," said Jim.

They looked at one another. The newspaper blew away. Quietly they got into their cars and departed. As

George left the parking lot he noticed a small turban clad figure sitting cross-legged on a blanket with an old brass begging bowl in front of him. He looked up at George and winked.

The Return of the Bambino

Tom O'Donnell, the new Sox General Manager, parked his BMW in Fenway Park's executive lot. He hauled himself out of his car and grunted at the articles spread over the back seat. The Boston press was trumpeting the fact that he was too young and lacked sufficient big league experience to take the Sox to the playoffs, let alone win another World Series.

He ran his fingers through his crew cut, shrugged, and trashed the clippings. He headed for his office overlooking the newly-renovated and expanded grandstand seats in right field to the left of Pesky's pole. The skies were gray. The Sox had a scheduled twi-night twin bill against the Tampa Bay Rays. He feared it would rain.

Stopping at the little coffee shop in the building, he took his usual seat at the counter.

The petite redheaded waitress looked at him: "What'll it be?"

He grinned at her and ordered his usual: two sugar donuts and an extra large dark roast coffee. He sighed. Just as they had every other summer, the Sox had begun to lose ground in the win column. Since the All Star break they seemed to have misplaced the killer instinct that keeps a great team winning.

Though their bullpen remained effective, their big

bats had retreated south of the border after losing two out of three games in Texas. The Tigers, White Sox, Angels, and Mariners had begun to look invincible. Each club had made some shrewd trades and picked up seasoned bats. Tom knew that Sox fans were getting restless waiting for him to make his move.

"Should I pick up the veteran first-baseman just optioned by the Cubs? He's cheap money and maybe had enough pop left in his bat to help win a few. There's an open spot on the roster."

The waitress eyed him as he mumbled to himself. She held up the coffeepot and raised her eyebrows. He shook his head.

The Yankees were the bane of Tom's existence. While the Sox floundered, barely holding onto first place in the AL East, they won in Kansas City and were only two games back.

He wiped his fingers on his paper napkin and left a nice tip on the counter. As he stepped out onto the sidewalk, suddenly he was confronted by an old woman. Tom sidestepped quickly to avoid knocking her over. Swathed in silky black robes, she jingled with the little silver charms that dangled from the edges. She smiled up at him. He looked down into a mouth that showed more gold than teeth.

"Alms for an old woman battered by life," she begged, extending her wrinkled palm. "You are good man, much good luck be for you! Cross my palm and see your wish come true."

"Yeah! Sure! And Manny's finally going to figure out how to play the wall in left." He laughed. Charitably, he reached into his pants pocket and pulled out a dollar bill. "Here," he said. "Take it and tell me what we have to do to win both games today against the Rays."

The woman snatched the money and made it disappear into the folds of her robes. "You want big wins today?" she chuckled.

"Yeah, that's the idea," Tom nodded, tight-lipped. He couldn't help but feel there was something strange, even mystical about her. It was almost as though he knew her and had talked to her many times before. But that made no sense. He'd never seen her in his life.

"Cross my palm four more times," she demanded, her dark eyes burned into his. As though in a trance he reached into his pocket and extracted four more bills.

He handed them to her. "What else can you tell me," he almost whispered.

"Here," she cackled. She extracted an old brass lamp from the folds of her robes. "Rub lamp three times and get free wish. Be careful what you wish. It will come true."

"Is that it? Five bucks for an old beat up brass lamp?"

She made a deep sound in her throat. "Lamp as old as pyramids," she assured him. "You'll see."

He couldn't help but grin. "So that's it? No more words of wisdom?"

She sighed, squinted upward and cackled. Then she raised her wrinkled arms into the air and slowly opened and closed her bony fingers. Almost immediately the sun burst through the clouds. *That was a pretty good trick*, he thought.

Tom looked at the lamp's odd markings. Maybe they represented an ancient forgotten language. But was it really old or just a knock-off from some factory in

Bayonne that specialized in fraud and broken dreams? As though reading his mind she raised her head toward the sky and mumbled something indecipherable.

"What's that? Say that again?" Tom said.

"Forget about the first-baseman from the Cubs," she said distinctly. "His bat's dead."

"Pick up that bat from the Cubs?" Larry, Tom's boss breezed into Tom's office. Tom shook his head. "Dead bat," he said.

"The Yankees will if we don't," Larry warned. "Better think it over. Once the Evil Empire grabs 'em, the press will have a field day at our expense."

"Let 'em," Tom said. He felt exasperated. He loved his job as Sox General Manager, but it was always the Yankees this, the Yankees that. He hated feeling threatened and intimidated by the Bronx Bombers. Certainly he didn't have to be reminded how badly the Red Sox Nation yearned for another World Series trophy.

Larry pointed at the lamp and laughed sarcastically. "Maybe if you rub that thing..."

"Sure!" Tom felt a little foolish. But baseball has always been prone to superstition. All sorts of oddities played their own peculiar role as harbingers of good luck: peculiarities in uniforms, custom-made bats, hairstyles, facial hair, tattoos, earrings, even thick gold chains and kitschy medallions.

Larry laughed again and from the hallway turned and called back to Tom. "Go ahead, rub it and see what happens. Way we've played recently, we've nothing to lose."

Tom closed his office door and returned to his desk.
He held the lamp and studied the strange hieroglyphics
etched into its bronzed copper. Absentmindedly, he
rubbed his right hand over its contour. A bright glowing
purple haze began to flow from its spout. He pushed
back his chair and stood up. The lamp fell from his
hand onto his desk. A vaguely human form clad in
bright robes, curved black slippers and a yellow turban
emerged from the swirling purple haze. All he could
think of was movies he'd seen of Aladdin.

"You've called Idries," a haughty voice yawned. "And
by the Will of the Great One, your wish will be
granted."

Tom's eyes bulged. "You a genie?"

"Definitions create limitations," Idries said. "Quickly
now, what is your wish? A chest full of gold? Always a
popular choice! Or perhaps the perennial castle and
harem of lovely beauties in Shangri La! Perfect for the
discriminating master."

"To win it all." Tom stammered, "for the Sox to win
the World Series again like we did back in '04."

"Really!" Idries wrinkled his noise.

"Our payroll's over the top, our gate receipts are
down. Our fans are exasperated! And worse, the press
has begun to call what we did in '04 a fluke."

"I see!" Idries stroked his chin.

Tom smiled, "Maybe we need to get Babe Ruth back
in a Red Sox uniform," he chuckled. "Could you do
that?"

"A most unusual request, I must say!" Idries planted
one foot firmly on the floor and slowly began to turn in

circles. Wisps of purple rose from his head and shoulders.

When he finally stopped he looked at Tom and nodded. "Yes! That is possible. But within certain limitations," he said wisely.

"What limitations?"

"Nothing all that difficult."

"Then make it happen." Tom urged. "Bring the Bambino back to Boston!"

"That is your wish? Not gold, or a castle with delightful lovelies?"

Tom nodded. Nothing in the rulebook said he couldn't wish for something as improbable as this. Besides, what general manager would turn down such an opportunity? Surely Brian Cashman, his rival in New York, wouldn't. He could just imagine the Steinbrenner's family glee at having the Babe batting in the same lineup with Jeter, Cano, and A-Rod.

Idries waved a long bony finger. "A word of extreme caution! You must never repeat aloud the name 'Babe Ruth'!"

"Sure," Tom agreed without giving it any thought. "Just go get him."

"You must never say his name aloud," Idries reiterated. "Else all is irretrievably lost."

"Sure," Tom agreed.

"Despite all eventualities."

"Like what?" His voice cracked.

Idries paused. "From my paltry knowledge of the game today, I'd be watchful of meddlesome agents, a hawkish player's union, free agency, salary arbitration, a weak though nonetheless intrusive Commissioner's Office, odds makers, even possible Congressional investigations into baseball's odd antitrust exemptions. All of this tantalizes a media starved for the most minuscule of detail; and believe me, once he starts to hit his legendary home runs, they will flock."

"Then you stick around; be his agent and watch his back." Tom said breathlessly. "All you need to pull that off is cash, cigars, and plenty of second-rate French wine. He'll be known to everyone as George Herman."

Idries bowed. "So be it!" The purple haze began to reflect a myriad of colors infused with the sounds of bats hitting home runs and cheering fans and threaded with the scent of *sauerbraten*, beer, Bay Rum, peanuts and Cracker Jacks. From this whirling cyclone a human shape began to materialize. Within moments a youthful, muscular Babe Ruth, wearing only his underwear, tumbled onto the floor of Tom's office.

"Where'd my silk pajamas go," the Babe cried out angrily? Then in total confusion he stared at Tom and growled, "Who are you and where in blazes am I?"

"I'm the Red Sox GM, and you're in my office at Fenway Park," Tom explained to a bewildered and disoriented Babe. "A genie brought you to the year 2007 to help us win the World Series. But that's our absolute secret. No one can ever get wind of that."

The Babe ignored his words. He wrinkled his nose. "I just woke up in my farmhouse in Sudbury. I'm brushing my teeth. My wife's Helen's cooking breakfast. It's 1918. We just won the World Series. Now I'm where? What gives?"

"Back in Boston, eighty nine years later." Idries clarified. He strolled over to him and held out his hand. "And it's a pleasure to meet you George Herman, and to serve exclusively as your agent and confidant."

"I haven't died or anything?" Idries shook his head. "I'm still who I always was, only I'm here in the future now instead of back there then?" The Babe rubbed at his chin.

"Well put!" Idries nodded, snapped his fingers and looked deeply into The Babe's eyes. "I'd say you've made a perfectly splendid transition. You're happy to be here."

The Babe blinked, sighed and shrugged. "So what's in all this hocus pocus for me?"

"In a nutshell," Tom said, "back in your time you're going to get sold to the Yankees."

"Play for them bums?" The Babe let loose a truckload of expletives.

"Afraid so," Tom agreed. "Harry Frazee needed more cash to finance his Broadway musicals. So he busts up the Sox."

"So that's why, before, the bum went and traded Tris Speaker to Cleveland!"

Tom nodded. "Baseball's always been a business. But once you hit New York your popularity soars and you save baseball from the stigma of the Black Sox gambling scandal."

The Babe clenched his fist. "Them guys finally pull a fast one on Charley Comiskey. Treats his players like dirt. Holds back on their salaries, wouldn't even give his ace Eddie Cocotte money when his kid got sick and needed a doctor. Never shows no respect, not even for Shoeless Joe. Owners!"

Tom nodded sympathetically. "You'll become known worldwide as The Sultan of Swat, make more money than any other player in the game, and emerge as the greatest home-run hitter of all time." He saw no need to mention Hank Aaron or Barry Bonds.

"Frazee's a creep." The Babe muttered. "So he'll railroad me to the Yankees just so he gets champagne money for his fillies." Another truckload of expletives poured out. "I just want to go home."

"And you shall, no doubt about that at all," Idries assured him. "As soon as this brief adventure is concluded and without losing one moment from your time either." He said hypnotically. "After all, life is but a dream, and wherever you go, well, there you are."

"OK," Tom said. Here's the deal. Finish out our season, play the outfield, lead us to another World Championship. The dead ball is on its way out. Play for us and you'll get used to hitting fastballs plus all sorts of finesse pitching."

"Go tell that one to Walter Johnson!"

"Once you hit the Bronx you'll become legend, dazzle fans and turn the new Yankee Stadium into the House that Ruth Built."

Larry lurched into his office, saw the young George Herman standing there in his underwear and stopped abruptly. Tom looked around. Idries had vanished. Tom saw a faint purple haze emanating from the lamp's spout.

"Boss, I want you to meet our new rookie phenom." Tom took a deep breath. "George Herman, meet the

Boss. He gives the orders around here." Then he picked up his phone and barked, "Where are those uniforms I ordered yesterday? What's going on with you in the clubhouse?"

Larry studied The Babe's face. "Something about you rings a definite bell."

"How about ordering me some breakfast?" the Babe demanded. "A side of bacon, half a dozen fried eggs over light, coffee with extra cream."

Larry frowned and stared at Tom. "Real rude for a rookie. Guess where he grew up, humility went out the window before the second grade, assuming he got that far."

The Babe cracked a grin. "Learned a lot more than hitting at the orphanage in Baltimore."

"So without telling me, you up and pluck this bozo out of the boonies?"

"Believe me, he'll impress you," Tom said.

"He better!" Larry said bluntly. "Let's just hope he can hit and run half as good as Carl Crawford."

"Never heard of the bum," the Babe said gruffly. "Me, I hit real good and dance the bases faster than any hoofer you've got stashed over in Scollay Square."

Larry's face reddened. There was a slight tremor in his voice. "Young man," he said, "there's a thin line between arrogance and confidence. Around here, it takes MVP stats for even the slightest hint of arrogance to be tolerated."

The Babe laughed and put a large beefy arm around Larry's shoulders. "Watch me hit 'em into the bleachers and you'll be honored to iron my shirt collars." He winked at Larry. "Then we can talk about my bonus."

At the batting cage, Tom introduced George Herman to his field manager. "Tito, I'd like you to play him today,"

Tito nodded reluctantly. "Hot prospect?"

"More than you could ever imagine. Sit someone down and start the kid in right."

"You sure?" Tito asked. "Drew's finally feeling well enough to play."

"Trust me," Tom said. "He's got a magical bat."

"Any chance we can see it in action?"

"Sure! Put him in the batting cage and think World Series."

"Amigo," Tito called to one of his relievers. "Throw a few to this new kid."

Amigo's face reddened. He shook his head indignantly. "My contract says I no throw batting practice, Señor. Call my agent!"

"Pull that kind of mouth on Billy Carrigan and he'd end up in traction for a month," the Babe mumbled.

"Who's Carrigan?" Tito asked.

"Nobody important." Tom said. "Just some hot head coach in Double A."

Tito turned to his reliable veteran. "Curt, pitch a few to this kid."

"Sure," Curt walked out to the mound. The Babe wiggled a menacing 36-inch Louisville Slugger and crowded the plate. Curt fired a high hard one dangerously close to his head up around his eyes. Rather than fall away the Babe turned and dropped a perfect bunt down the third base line. A few of the vets around the cage hooted.

"Beginners' luck," one cried.

"Like to see Manny do that," another laughed.

Curt rubbed up a new baseball and threw a changeup that flirted with the outside corner of the plate. The Babe easily drove it over the Green Monster in left.

"See what I mean?" Tom grinned at Tito. The manager nodded and rolled his eyes.

Curt took off his cap, mopped his brow, and grinned at the Babe. "Where'd you learn to hit like that?"

"At the orphanage," the Babe shouted. "Been swinging lumber like that since I was six."

Local Fox TV sportscaster Scarlet Dickens sashayed up to Tom and winked. Her Red Sox T shirt was tight across her admirable chest. "How about a chance to interview this fabulous new rookie?"

His old buddy Chris Penny, Sports Editor for the *Rockland Picayune* looked up from his laptop and grinned. "He's something, isn't he? I'm trying to find his stats from the minors."

"Leave the kid be!" Tom said rudely to Scarlet. "He's off-limits." He knew all about Scarlet and her late night interviews: how nine times out of ten her intimate soirées ended up at her Commonwealth Avenue penthouse. She seemed to have homed right in on the Babe. Idries was right. Tom realized there would be a media stampede once George Herman started hitting them into the seats.

"This guy's a keeper, huh?" She winked again and batted her eyelashes. "Freedom of the Press, sweetie." She blew Tom a kiss and wandered off.

Curt took a couple of deep breaths, went into his full wind-up and delivered a deceptively low change-up that teased the outside corner of the plate. The Babe grinned stepped into it and parked it deep into the back row of the center-field bleachers. By now everyone on the team was watching with newfound admiration. Other members of the press gathered to gape at this new green kid. It was like the resurrection of the Great White Hope.

Larry trudged out onto the field and took Tom aside. "Who's this Idries character? Says he's George Herman's agent and handed me a silver goblet of real good Rothschild. Then told me we need to talk about a signing bonus!"

"That's him," Tom nodded. He wished Scarlet could somehow be distracted.

"Your kid's got it all," Chris folded up his laptop and smiled at Tom. "Where'd you find him? I couldn't come up with anything from the minors."

"State secret," Tom smiled. "Sometimes it's better not to dig."

"Go ahead, tramp all over my bread and butter. Deny me my best story since my Barry Bonds blog drew national attention."

The Babe stormed over to Tom. His eyes squinted up, his cheeks flushed. "You got some weird colored guys out there! Baseball's supposed to be a white man's game! If Cap Anson took one look at this ragtag outfit, he'd shut down the whole shootin' match."

"Easy!" Tom prayed for a miracle.

Idries appeared and looked hypnotically into the Babe's eyes. "Life is truly blind of all skin color." He touched the Babe lightly on the shoulder.

The Babe shook his head, blinked and scratched his chest. David Ortiz left the dugout and headed over. "You got it good with that swing," he grinned. "Welcome!"

But rather than reply the Babe nodded curtly and headed into the dugout. Idries walked over to Scarlet. He handed her a goblet of wine and soon they were engaged in animated conversation.

"So where'd you find him?" Chris Penny asked with a grin. "In the middle of a Klan meeting?"

The Sox took both ends of the twi-night double-header from the Rays, 6 - 2 and 5 - 1. In the opener The Babe went 3 for 4 with two homers and a double before being twice intentionally passed by. His only out was a screaming liner stabbed against the wall in center by B.J. Upton. In the nightcap the Babe flew out deep to right, doubled, homered, and again was intentionally passed by.

Tom's cell phone rang as he entered the clubhouse. "You're a genius," Larry laughed. "That kid looked great out there." He paused and Tom could envision the furrows on his boss's brow. "It's funny, but I just can't figure out what it is about him that makes him seem so familiar to me."

"All those guys from A-Ball look alike." Tom quipped. "I just hope he doesn't eat us out of hot dogs and soda pop. According to Tito he put away a dozen dogs, and a six pack of cola between games."

"Just a growing boy," Larry laughed.

The rhythmic beat of sultry Latin music wafted throughout the clubhouse. Chatting affably, Idries served a goblet of red wine to Chris Penny. Scarlet Dickens entered and made a beeline over to the Babe. Hurriedly, Tom concluded his conversation with Larry and moved in their direction.

"George Herman, honey," she drawled. "You're my new hero!" She flipped her blond hair and wriggled her shoulders. "What say you and little ol' Ms. Scarlet here sneak away and spend some quality time together?" She tilted her head and blinked her baby blues.

The Babe raised his eyebrows and looked her over: "You always dress in a man's suit coat and trousers with your belly exposed that way? Ain't ya kinda chilly?"

"Why, George Herman," she giggled. "Do tell how you like your ladies dressed." Her eyes flirted mischievously.

"Like a respectable lady!" The Babe shot back. "Trussed up in a fancy lace corset with plenty of bustle showing off her caboose."

Scarlet gulped and wrinkled her nose. "And what's your ideal woman like?"

"I'll take one who can hoe her own potatoes, darn a man's socks and feed him a good breakfast without complainin' about her lumbago, keep her mind to herself and not get heated up over all that suffragette malarkey."

Scarlet's face reddened. Apparently the Babe had touched a nerve. "You want to take away a woman's right to vote?" She yanked open her laptop and began to type furiously.

"Didn't know they ever got it," the Babe snorted.

"What do women know about politics anyhow? Best they stay home, do the wash, and care for the children. Next thing you know they'll want their own bank accounts and to go out and drive their own motorcars."

Scarlet's voice rose several octaves catching the attention of Chris Penny and Idries. They turned and looked in her direction.

She glared at the Babe. "Has anyone ever told you how unattractive a male chauvinist can be?"

"What's attractive about me is my bat," the Babe assured her. "That's what makes the ladies sit up and take notice."

Hastily Tom walked over, put his arm around the Babe and guided him away from a rather flushed Scarlet. "Come on, George, let's zip over to the Top of The Hub."

Scarlet punched a series of numbers into her cell phone. "This is Scarlet Dickens here at Fenway Park," she said sharply. "The Sox just brought up a throwback to the Old Stone Age. Believe me, King Kong has more class than this rookie. But tonight, George Herman hit three homers and has everyone around here talking World Series..."

As they drove down Commonwealth Avenue, Tom said, "When you're around press people, try to just talk about the game. Don't mention personal stuff that might give you away. Not that anyone would ever believe it! But let's play it safe. Remember, you're just a green rookie up from Double A and glad to be in the Bigs!"

"All those kids look like immigrants." The Babe peered at the students gathered outside clubs in Kenmore Square. "Look at the tattoos on that kid's arm!

The weird hair! The short skirts! Why, that girl's downright exposed! And that one's britches are torn at the knees and look like they'll fall off. Can't any of them afford decent clothes?"

"It's the grunge look," Tom laughed. "Highly fashionable amongst students these days! You wouldn't believe how expensive that look can be. All those tears are hand crafted."

"So this is the future!" The Babe marveled. "Lights on all night long. Kids pay a fortune to look poor. Everyone's got fold up telephones in their pockets! Motor cars that move as fast as trains."

Tom took a right on Mass Ave. and then a left onto Huntington. "Will you look at that!" The Babe stared upward at the Prudential complex. "I never saw buildings up so high before. Hope it doesn't fall down if it gets too windy."

Back in his condo at the Pru, Tom ensconced the Babe in his spare bedroom. Soon the Bambino was snoring loudly, although not before he had consumed a half-pound of Italian sausage, several generous helpings of potato salad and three bottles of ale. Wide-eyed with bewilderment, Tom sat on his couch and tried to relax. But then his doorbell rang.

"Kinda late!" Tom yawned through the intercom.

"Better let me in!" Chris Penny cried out. "Scarlet's on the warpath and out for blood!" Moments later the Sports Editor for the *Rockland Picayune* made a beeline for Tom's high definition TV. Scarlet Dickens had just begun her late night Sports Wrap Up.

"Who's this mysterious throwback to the Old Stone

Age?" she asked as she kicked off her show. "What's up with Sox GM Tom O'Donnell? Why is he so close-mouthed about where he found the chauvinistic George Herman? The way that ape hits home runs, possibly he's King Kong reborn! What's up, Tom? Why no minor league stats any of us here at Foxy Sports can uncover?" Her eyes blazed from the screen. "Maybe he's a robot you downloaded from the Internet!"

But that wasn't the end of her tirade. "Joining me now is George Herman's equally mysterious agent, Idries Folly." The camera showed a grinning Idries clad in a tan Armani suit, complete with silky Red Sox Nation ascot. "Ok, Idries, come clean and tell us the truth about this kid!"

Idries smiled playfully into the camera. His bright blue eyes pools of fathomless depth, he exuded disarming charm. He opened his palms and gently waved them over Scarlet's head. "Yes, he is a fine and gifted young boy. Yes, he will lead the Red Sox to ultimate victory. It is in the stars. Yes, he is free to hit home runs across the country."

"What's up with him?" Chris Penny asked. "It's like he's putting her to sleep."

Tom could hardly believe what he was seeing.

"Free to hit home runs across the country," Scarlet repeated dreamily. She seemed to have dropped her tirade and forgotten her earlier accusations.

"Yes! That's right!" Idries smiled. Again he gently waved his hands as though conducting an invisible orchestra.

"It's like he's got her under a spell," Chris Penny shook his head, went to the fridge, got two beers and handed one to his friend.

Tom nodded.

"Wish she responded to me that way," Chris said woefully. "I keep thinking someday we'll become an item!"

"Talk to Idries," Tom said half seriously. "He seems to have a way with women. Anyway," he hoisted his beer, "here's to the future!"

Over the next few weeks the Sox behaved like acrobatic magicians, making one incredible play after another. At the plate everyone tore the cover off the ball. The Babe's magical intensity was contagious.

It was during the final home stand against the Yankees that Scarlet again confronted Tom and Idries. They were sitting in the executive rooftop boxes eating crab-meat and asparagus quiche.

"Tell me who you are?" Scarlet demanded of Idries. "No one in the Bigs has ever heard of you."

Idries beamed. His tanned dome emanated a faint purple glow. "I'm the CEO of Jinn Inc," he said simply. He looked deeply into her eyes. "Yes, we specialize in fulfilling dreams."

Scarlet swayed and stifled a yawn. "I just love George Herman," she admitted. "But he pays me no mind at all."

"He's got to think about the game," Tom said lamely.

"Have no regrets my dear," Idries said sympathetically. "Your true love patiently awaits. And he is closer than you might ever suspect."

The Sox took the first two games in their crucial final three-game series against the Yankees. The Babe clouted three homers and finally Yankee manager Joe Torre ordered him intentionally walked whenever he came to bat.

During the top of the ninth inning in Game Three, Shill momentarily lost control. His change-ups were too high and both Jeter and A-Rod spanked doubles off the Green Monster in left. Matsui homered. Posada singled through the hole at second. Tito called time and trotted out to the mound. The catcher and second baseman joined him.

"Stay loose, Shill," he urged. "We're still up by three."

"I spoke to my broker between innings," Shill whined. "He said my portfolio could be in jeopardy. He said sell now and never mind heavy capital gains."

"That's tough!" His catcher sympathized.

"I put my money in municipals," the young second baseman said. The home plate umpire made his way to the mound.

Tito patted Shill's shoulder. "Better call him from the clubhouse. Wouldn't want you taking a loss." Pap came in from the bullpen, put out the fire and got the save. The Sox swept the series and had first place locked up. The American League East was theirs.

American League Pennant. Earlier they had put away the Yankees in five. Becket and Dice K were slated to start the first two games of the World Series at Fenway against the Mets.

Tom's doorbell rang. He opened his door. Chris Penny stood in the hall. "Come in," Tom said.

Chris walked in and threw himself onto the couch. "I took your advice and asked her out to dinner," he said breathlessly. "She said, 'Sure why not!' which isn't exactly an invitation for anything much." He sighed. "Sounds like love at first sight, doesn't it?"

"You've been infatuated with her ever since she joined the sports staff over at Foxy."

"Seems unfair for me to have to pick up the tab though," Chris complained. "I mean, she makes five to six times what I pull in."

Tom pulled out his wallet and peeled off three big ones. "Top of the Hub," he said, handing them to Chris. "On me." He wondered what it was about Scarlet Dickens that turned Chris into a groveling adolescent.

"Nice!" Chris said breathlessly. "Gee, thanks, maybe that'll impress her. I think she hardly knows I'm alive. So when do I get my exclusive interview with George Herman?"

"As soon as we clinch it and the fat lady sings."

"Didn't you hear, the fat lady's on a diet doing TV spots for Weight Droppers."

"Call Top of the Hub and make your reservation." Tom waved at him, "And get outta here."

Chris nodded, jumped up off the couch, and hurried out the door.

Idries appeared in Tom's office and bowed. Clad in his fashionable Armani suit, a sky blue shirt, and his silky Red Sox Nation ascot he carried a magnum of rare French champagne. "With the compliments of the Empress Josephine," he smiled. "She and her corpulent little Corporal send you their warmest personal regards."

"Don't pop that bottle," Tom cautioned. Visions of Slaughter scoring while Pesky held the ball in '46, or the Mets erupting and Buckner missing Wilson's seeing eye grounder to first base flashed through his mind. "Remember what Yogi, said, 'It ain't over 'till it's over.'"

"That's all quite true," the genie pursed his lips, but I'd say that in our most unusual fashion we've put that old curse to rest. You've got clear sailing until the ultimate realization of your specific wish. Then," he grinned, "the sky's the limit."

"What do you mean?" Tom asked. In the back of his mind a warning bell sounded.

"Significant roster changes to benefit the game," Idries smiled. "I have been studying baseball's statistical history."

"Come again?"

"Judging by the George Herman's popularity in Boston, could you imagine how well-received Wagner would be in Pittsburgh? Or Cobb in Detroit? Speaker in Cleveland? Even Walter Johnson's triumphant return to Washington. Think of the pandemonium over DiMaggio's return to the Yankees or Ted Williams and Lefty Grove rejoining our own George Herman here at Fenway?"

He put the tips of his fingers together and grinned widely at Tom. "Assuming of course that ownership is willing to make an even more sizable investment. But think of the benefits. No steroids to get in the way."

"You could do that?" Tom's eyes widened. "Stretch yourself back in time and bring back the greatest Hall of Fame players still in their prime?"

Idries fluttered his fingers and little sparks flew off the ends. "Simply a matter of reversal of energy fields. Restructure light and time. A dib of Einstein, a dab of Hawking—a far simpler task than materializing gold out of nowhere for some greedy old caliph in ancient Mesopotamia."

Tom gulped. Maybe Idries had been out of his bottle for a little too long. He could just imagine Ty Cobb flying into second, spikes high, taking out a would-be infielder; or some deadball-era pitcher deliberately hurling a high, hard bean ball at a batter's head. He shivered. Back then, baseball was a brutal, ruthless game with plenty of alcohol but no player's union to smooth things over.

However, Tom couldn't help but imagine the excitement at the next GM's meeting if the Tigers signed a miraculous hitting, base-stealing kid named Tyrus Raymond, or if the White Sox brought up a repentant rookie nicknamed Shoeless Joe. "And nothing can keep this from happening? Like what if God didn't go for the idea?"

Idries raised his brows and blushed. "I doubt in the scheme of things it would even be noticed."

"And Jinn Inc. represents everyone?"

"Exactly!" With a smile and a wave of his hand he conjured up three more magnums of rare French champagne. "But best if mum's the word."

The next morning the Babe bounded into Tom's office and looked demandingly at Idries. "Can't you bring Helen back here too? It's lonely every night sleeping by myself in his spare bedroom. I mean, we're married after all."

"You got to think about the game." Tom said stoically.

"What dreams may come," Idries smiled at the Babe. "How inconsiderate of me to deny you your marital bliss."

"Yeah," the Babe agreed. "Like when there's no knockwurst to go alongside a mountain of mashed potatoes."

Chris Penny and Scarlet Dickens entered the elevator at the Pru. Chris pushed the button for the celebrated Top of The Hub. He felt like a schoolboy on his first date. Nervously Scarlet consulted her watch.

"Three-plus hours till game time," Chris hoped he sounded debonair and nonchalant.

"I'd like a few words from Becket before his first pitch." Scarlet sounded like a NASCAR driver about to accelerate off the starting line.

"Press ban till after the game," Chris said. "Always that way at World Series time."

"Tom owes me one," she huffed. Mid-way up to the restaurant the elevator lurched, swung on its cable, and came to a grinding halt. The lights flickered and went out. Chris and Scarlet fell against one another. Slowly they untangled and stood up.

"You ok?" he asked.

"Do something!" She demanded shrilly.

"Like what?" He guessed they were somewhere between the fortieth and fiftieth floor.

"Get us out of here! I've got to get to Fenway!" She snapped open her cell phone but it was dead.

"I don't think they work in elevators." Chris had a terrible sinking feeling. She probably felt this was entirely his fault.

"There must be an emergency escape hatch, something to push open." She tipped her head back and stared upward. "Up there, push on the top and get it open. Then climb up the shaft and bring back help." She made it sound so easy.

"You want me to risk my life?" Chris's knees trembled. Heights were not his strong suit.

She huffed impatiently. "That's what people do when they get stuck in elevators."

He took a deep breath. What was it about her? His rational side questioned the smitten schoolboy. "Ok, I'll do it but on one condition!"

"Men!" She sighed. "Whatever sneaky little ploy you're thinking won't work in an elevator."

"Marry me!" he blurted. "I've been in love with you since the first day we met."

"Marry you?" Her voice rose. "We're stuck in an elevator and you're proposing? How can I possibly think about anything but getting out of here!"

He sighed, shook his head, and jumped toward the roof. "Here, take this," she said. Maybe he was imagining it but her voice seemed to have softened. He wished it had been a kiss but instead she put a mini flashlight in his hand. "Don't lose it."

On his third try he managed to push open the top. Now they could make their voices heard, and in a short time they were rescued and on their way to Fenway.

The Mets took Game One by a bundle. Tom Glavin prevailed. Josh Becket gave up four homers and was in no mood for any post-game interviews. The Sox committed four fielding errors. But worse, The Babe struck out three times.

In Game Two, Wakefield's knuckle ball was flat and off the plate. Reluctantly, Tito pulled him before the end of the fifth. Timlin came in and hit a batter, his curve-ball and slider totally ineffective. But worse, George Herman seemed in a terrible slump, striking out six times in his first eight Series at-bats. Red Sox Nation began to mumble. The Sox were down by five.

"Maybe we need a new manager, Tom!" Larry said in his usual, over-reactive way. "Maybe the pressure's getting to Tito."

"Got anyone better in mind? How about we resurrect Casey Stengel?" Tom joked, masking his concern.

"What's wrong with our rookie sensation?" Larry asked devouring another crab-meat roll.

"He misses his missus."

"Then find 'em another one," Larry grumbled. "It's the World Series, anything goes."

Tom nodded, stood and headed for the rooftop boxes. Astonished, he saw an inebriated Idries, his arms around a pair of adoring buxom young ladies singing "Take Me Home From The Ballgame." His usual purple glow had turned dark muddy green.

Firmly, Tom took the genie's elbow and led him away.

"Buy me some hummus and baba ganoush," Idries sang off key.

"Sober up!" Tom shouted, pulling him inside his office. "Do something magical and get back your purple glow. The Babe's not hitting for beans."

Idries blinked. "Abracadabra." He giggled drunkenly repeating it several times.

"Come up with something better," Tom scolded.

"You've lost your focus and so has everyone else."

Idries frowned.

"Drink this!" Tom handed him a tall glass of water.

"Whazzat?" The genie wrinkled his aristocratic nose but took the water and swallowed it down.

"Everything started to fall apart the minute you opened that fancy French booze."

Idries blinked several times, rubbed his well-upholstered belly, and burped. Then he smiled and nodded. Slowly his purple glow returned. He took several deep breaths, rubbed his hands together briskly and stamped each foot three times.

Suddenly the fans began to cheer. Down by three, two outs, bottom of the eighth, Manny doubled. The lackadaisical crowd jumped to its feet. Ortiz singled him home. Drew tripled scoring Ortiz. Then Lugo singled, scoring Drew. Yuke doubled. The Mets made a pitching change.

On the first pitch The Babe hit a towering home run. Tom high-fived Idries and they headed for the Executive Boxes. Pap closed out the ninth for his first World Series save. The magic was back.

The Sox took two out of three in New York, and after an off-day back at Fenway defeated the Mets 4-0 for the World Championship. Dice K pitched a near perfect game, allowing only a bunt single in the third and a late inning double in the corner by the bullpen in right center. The Babe homered twice, in the fifth and again in the home half of the eighth. The post-game World Series hoopla was incredible. All of Boston but most especially Kenmore Square was ablaze with confetti and delirious fans.

Sipping Napoleon brandy, Idries toasted Tom. "I'm proud of your astute use of magical ways."

For the first time in months, Tom felt relaxed.

Larry breezed in. "Just got off the phone with Mr. Bluster himself," he boasted. "Pulled off the trade of the century!" He laughed and waved a Havana cigar like a baton. "He's giving us A-Rod, Jeter, Posoda and Matusi for George Herman and a couple of farm hands to be named later."

Tom gulped. "You'd trade him to the Yankees?"

A faint smile whisked across Idries' lips.

"Listen, Tom. Sure, the kid looked great but the business of baseball is business. Right now we're on top, and with consistent pitching and strong hitting we'll stay up there and contend. Plus this way we get the heart of the Yankees lineup. The fans got their wish: a second World Series for Boston, But forty million for him next year puts us too deep into the luxury tax."

Tom gulped hard. He sat bolt upright and clutched at his hair. "But don't you realize what you've done?" And before he could stop himself he said, "You've traded away Babe Ruth!"

Idries sighed. As though on cue he began to fade away. "History has a curious way of repeating," he murmured. Then he vanished.

Larry looked confused. "Huh?" He shook his head. "Was someone just in here?"

Tom's eyes filled with tears. "Sometimes when you get what you wish for, it only makes you want more."

Back in his apartment at the Pru, Tom put the old

brass lamp on the mantelpiece next to his autographed picture of Ted Williams. Feeling lost, he wandered through the rooms. The Babe's loud silk pajamas from Banana Republic were still tossed over the hamper in the bathroom. His doorbell rang. Chris Penny rushed in.

The jovial Sports Editor was breathless with excitement. "Scarlet's going to meet my mom for brunch on Sunday," he gasped. He bounded into the kitchen, opened the fridge and helped himself to a beer. "I'm supposed to meet her folks over Thanksgiving. I've been invited to the family plantation in Kentucky. Thanks to you, we're finally an item."

"Nice," Tom smiled. "Dinner at the Top of the Hub can be magical."

"Especially when you get there via the elevator shaft," Chris laughed.

"Huh?"

"Later," Chris smiled. "Let's go grab that rookie sensation of yours and celebrate."

"He's gone." Tom said ruefully.

Chris stared at Tom. His eyes widened. "What? Where!" He blinked and shook his head. "Did he go on a binge? Do we need to go looking for him? Did some teeny bopper drag him off?"

Tom shook his head and fought back tears. "Where indeed? My guess is back somewhere in time." He could barely speak.

Chris clapped him on the back. "Aw, he was just another player. Good, but hey, they're around. Listen, why so glum? You just won yourself a World Series! Most GM's would be floating in Champagne by now."

"It's a long story," Tom said. "Let's go get some

lobsters and I'll tell you all about it."

Chris's phone rang. He opened it. "I'm at Tom's at
the Pru. Your place? Just us? I'm on my way!" He folded
his phone and grinned. "The little woman. Tell me later,
ok?" he called over his shoulder as he headed for the
elevator.

Tom sighed. He took a beer from the fridge, flipped
off the cap and held it up. "Here's to you, George
Herman Ruth." A vision of Idries flashed into his mind.
He set down the beer and picked up the lamp. Was the
dream really over? He rubbed it. For a moment a wisp
of purple haze lingered at the tip. Then it faded.

In their Sudbury farmhouse Helen was cooking
breakfast. The Babe lumbered into the kitchen. "I had
the craziest dream." He scooped her up and kissed her.
"I was in the future and I hit the winning home run that
won us the World Series. But it was weird. The buildings
were way taller, and everyone kept tiny phones attached
to their belts. The women were bossy and acted like they
thought they ruled the world."

Helen smiled and hugged her handsome husband.
"Next time don't drink so much lager before bedtime."
She served him his usual six egg onion and cheese
omelet with bacon and knockwurst. "They say President
Wilson doesn't look so well." But the Babe's nose was
buried in an article on the sports page of the morning
paper. It hinted that he might soon be traded to the
Yankees. Somehow that didn't surprise him.

The Family Portrait

Rudy was a quiet, sensitive only child of seven who lived with his mother, father and grandparents. He spent all his free time sketching and painting. Sadly, this annoyed his family because they didn't like his pictures. "I would never frame and hang anything like that in *my* home," said his mother, pointing to a scrawly swirl of loops with faces in it.

"It has no sense of perspective whatsoever," complained his father.

His mother's taste in art ran to trendy floral designs, old barns, and pretty children. Rudy's art embarrassed her. As soon as he'd finish a picture she'd whisk it away and hide it in a far corner of the basement.

That didn't bother Rudy. He laughed when she got upset at his sketch of her looking like a cactus with big lumpy feet, a distorted chin, and an eye where her ear should have been.

"He takes after your side of the family," said his father. He didn't appreciate Rudy's pictures of him looking like an enormous insect twisted into a banana peel.

"Not mine," she huffed. "They had good taste. He must take after yours."

"His trees look like they're falling down," Grandfather complained. "And what kind of an animal is that misshapen creature with seven legs?"

Rudy's mother sighed. "He must need therapy."

"Look into psychological testing," nodded the grandfather. "Once a mental defect is discovered these days, it can be knocked clear out of a child's head." He made a sour face. "Look at this! My grandson portrays me as half frog and half giraffe!"

"Yes, something is certainly wrong!" agreed his grandmother. "He titled that *Grandma!*" She pointed to a picture of a scrawny black cat with three eyes, dangling ears, a wobbly chin, and thick hairy sprouts leaping from two bulbous nostrils.

"Your chin's not quite like that," Grandfather assured her. "And your nose only bulges that way when you eat too much."

She frowned. "Thanks." Then she pointed and laughed at a picture of a scarecrow with a square face in an over-sized head, stuck onto long, spindly legs, simply entitled *Dad.*

The next day an excited Rudy came home from school with a flyer announcing an art contest for Earth Day. Large cash prizes would be awarded to winners from each grade, as well as the opportunity to be exhibited at the Fine Arts Museum. Rudy was so happy. Although he had never been to a museum, he felt as though his paintings belonged in them.

He spent all his free time creating his new Earth Day masterpiece.

"Don't even show it to us," said his father.

His mother frowned," we most certainly don't want to see it!"

His grandparents avoided him in the family room while he worked on it.

Rudy paid them no attention. He focused his concentration on his picture, worked diligently, and proudly took it to school the day of the exhibit.

That afternoon his parents received a nervous phone call from his teacher. "You must come immediately! Please!"

His alarmed parents looked at one another. "What trouble could he have caused with that terrible picture?"

Upon arriving they were greeted by his teacher and the school principal. Standing with them was a tall, distinguished gentleman, the Director of the Fine Arts Museum. Behind them on the wall, with a large splashy gold star next to it, was Rudy's painting entitled *Family Portrait*.

His father looked more like a wild bull than a man; his mother appeared as three twisted sticks within small bubbling circles, and his grandparents as two horned beasts from ancient mythology. Each held an enormous trash bag filled with litter.

"Your son is a genius," the Director said. "Not since Picasso has there been anything this original in modern art."

His parents gulped.

Rudy sat nearby quietly working away at another picture.

The principal beamed. "What wonderful parents you two are to have inspired your son at such an early age to express his creativity so freely. On behalf of our school, I thank you for encouraging his true gifts."

His mother gulped again.

His father coughed.

"Furthermore," the Director said, "we will buy

everything he has done so far and in return create for him a trust fund of a million dollars." He beamed. "A special exhibition will be announced."

The mother looked shocked. "They're at home," she said in a small voice.

"Where?" His father squeaked.

"Basement," she waved her hands helplessly.

"I can do lots more," Rudy looked up at the Director. "All I really want to do is paint and make pictures."

"Yes," his father proclaimed. "Our son is a great artist who obviously takes after my side of the family."

"No, mine of course," his mother contradicted.

"And we owe it all to Earth Day," his teacher said. "Had it not been for this student exhibit, Rudy's true talents might never have been recognized."

His father looked at his mother. His mother looked back at his father. Then, with tears in their eyes, they went to their son and hugged him.

"An artist," his mother said in a small voice.

"A million-dollar trust," said his father.

And from that day on, Rudy spent all of his free time painting, unless of course he was practicing on his electric guitar or outside playing with his friends.

Mr. Perkins and the Squirrels

Ever since that dreadful wallet incident, reality to Mr. Perkins seemed more than just a bit askew. Suddenly, without warning, people would appear to him transformed into horned beasts or bird-like creatures. At church his minister occasionally looked like a spotted owl or, at that climactic moment of his sermon, a bald eagle. At the department store the women selling home appliances resembled a gigantic green bug. When these peculiar shape shifting events or, worse in his mind, hallucinations occurred, Mr. Perkins could only squeeze shut his eyes and wish that they'd just stop and go away.

The incident with the squirrels began at the monthly meeting of his Neighborhood Watch. Ralph Hommack, the current Watch Chair, stood and, to Mr. Perkins' horror, took the shape of a large, hairy hedgehog. Even his voice had an odd squeak.

Not again, Mr. Perkins thought. *This can't go on, else I'd know for sure I've lost my mind or at least what's left of it.*

"So, we have agreement." Ralph Hommack banged his gavel. His voice was forceful and demanding. "The Watch will see to it that sufficient poisons are purchased and distribution will commence immediately. We'll drive those marauding critters back to Kingdom Come."

"Point of order," Eleanor Riley stood defiantly. "If you're trying to get rid of troublesome red squirrels just make sure you don't kill us as well."

Hommack's face reddened. "There's no turning back. Those critters are destroying property and making fools of us. We're getting known around town as a neighborhood soft on squirrels." He looked out at the weary homeowners. "And let me remind you all that the squirrel is cousin to the common rat."

That comment caused immediate uproar. Mr. Perkins wondered fancifully if there might be a Pied Piper handy. A man stood and shook his fist. "My garden's totally ruined."

"Mine too," a woman added. "My tomato patch looks like the remnants of World War Three."

"There'll be no harvest," a despondent homeowner complained.

"Blame it on development," another said. "What do you expect when wildlife is denied its usual habitant and forced out of the wild?"

"But isn't there a little park with trees by the shopping center," a woman asked. "Isn't that enough?"

Eleanor Riley stood and demanded the attention of the Chair. "I don't see why we can't remove them nonviolently, in a way that will keep our lawns and gardens safe for our children."

"In accordance with the Geneva Convention, I suppose," Hommack said sarcastically.

But several others showed their agreement, demanding some benign and safe elimination rather than the torturous brutality of spreading poison.

"How do you feel about this, Perkins?" Ralph looked his way, trying to maintain control of the meeting by shifting attention away from Eleanor and her prissy environmentalist crowd.

Mr. Perkins found himself standing amidst a pack of pecking chickens. Worse, the meeting room took on the appearance of a large, smelly chicken coop. He could taste his dismay. He had always felt ambivalent about squirrels. Occasionally they would eat from Helen's bird-feeder, but that was nothing compared to the current outburst of chaos. He'd never gotten that close to a squirrel. Truth be told, he preferred to remain inside rather than having to take on the rigors of the garden.

"I'm not really sure what to say," he started. "I am sure, however, that I'd rather we weren't exterminated prematurely and no doubt against our wishes by chemical poisons best not even used in war." He tried to smile. "Instead, were it just me, I'd suggest having lunch and breaking bread with their Board of Directors. Trying to understand their position and then working with development and patronage to hammer out some sort of compromise."

To him that seemed logical. It apparently worked for Congress that way, so why not with squirrels? Ralph stared at him in bewilderment. What he had just heard made no sense at all. What was Perkins getting at?

"And just how do you propose doing that?" a man asked. "Make a reservation for the Banquet Room?"

"Yes," Eleanor Riley said. "I hear what Mr. Perkins is recommending. We must form a committee and try to communicate directly with the Squirrel Deva. That way we can avoid unnecessary bloodshed."

"Who's Deva?" a woman asked.

"A what?" said another.

"Does he know his business?" A concerned voice asked.

"Mr. Perkins knows how we all think," Eleanor said. "His way is absolutely American."

"It's tried and true," the woman next to her said. "He seems so presidential."

Eleanor peered shyly at him. Sadly, what Mr. Perkins saw was not a middle-aged divorcée with a passion for rose bushes, but instead a benign dove fending off a raven with piercing eyes about to devour a small lamb.

Ralph Hommack banged his gavel. "One week," he said harshly. "You have seven days to come up with whatever agreement you want. But by next Friday unless things have changed, we're buying the pesticide to spread throughout the neighborhood." He banged his gavel and adjourned the meeting.

"You have such a way with words," Eleanor said. "You must join us when we communicate with the Squirrel Deva."

"I've never spoken squirrel," Mr. Perkins said, pleased to be asked. "But I wouldn't imagine it much different than talking turkey."

"If the good Lord could finish his work in six days," Mr. Perkins said to Eleanor Riley and her friend Maize Shaw over coffee at Eleanor's, "then that would seem sufficient time to set things straight with these unhappy squirrels."

"Assuming we know where to begin," Maize said. To Mr. Perkins' dismay, she resembled a fox terrier.

"You're so diplomatic, Eleanor cooed. What Mr. Perkins saw was a motherly dove fluttering her wings.

"They need their habitat," Maize said. "But now it's all suburban sprawl."

Eleanor peered at Mr. Perkins and smiled. "We're sure you'll lead us past these still waters."

Mr. Perkins looked thoughtful. "Obviously we can't give them back what's no longer there. Somehow we must make amends. Some sort of offering."

"I'm glad I'm not a squirrel." Maize's voice fell. "Compared to Daniel Boone's time, today's no picnic."

Eleanor nodded. "More trees. And the streams were clean."

"Maybe bottled water," Maize said. "As a show of good faith at least."

"And baskets of acorns," Eleanor said. "I'm sure we can find some on-line."

Googling acorns only brought up a pate from a small province in France. With shipping, the price was prohibitive.

"Maybe the bottled water will be enough," Mr. Perkins said.

Eleanor and Maize nodded enthusiastically.

"If we can find the Squirrel Deva you mentioned, I'm sure some diplomatic solution can be reached," Mr. Perkins said.

It was baffling that everyone with whom he came into contact looked like a creature rather than a human being. There had to be a reason for this but he couldn't fathom what it might be.

"I say we go into the wilderness and find her," Eleanor said. She sounded brave.

"What wilderness?" Maize asked. "We've nothing like that for miles and miles. There's only the little park behind the shopping center."

"Then as Ambassadors of Good Will we'll start there," Mr. Perkins said. "But first we must procure some bottled water."

After a light lunch, the intrepid trio of peace-keepers left for the shopping center and, as Mr. Perkins put it, "to attempt to break bread" with the Squirrel Deva.

Eleanor drove in and parked. The three climbed out of her Land Rover.

"Look," Maize said excitedly, "Mall Mart's having their big sale on ladies swimsuits. Oh, Mr. Perkins, please go ahead. We'll just be a minute and then we'll catch up with you."

"And we'll pick up the bottled water," Eleanor said.

Mr. Perkins nodded. He walked to the small park next to the Shopping Center. At that same moment an inebriated hobo stumbled into the park from the opposite direction.

Instead of a hobo, Mr. Perkins saw a huge hairy squirrel with red eyes and a certain slackness to its mouth, which Mr. Perkins attributed to hunger. Surely this must be the Squirrel Deva.

"Hello," Mr. Perkins said. "We come in peace."

The large Squirrel Deva squinted at him. "Whaaa?"

"I know! I know!" Mr. Perkins waved his hands. "And you've a perfect right to be disgruntled. I would be too if all my trees had been chopped down."

"Huh?"

"I know it's small consolation, but my colleagues will be bringing you bottled water."

Hearing the word water, the hobo's eyes widened. He made growling noises.

"I know just how you feel," Mr. Perkins said. "But if you will agree to our peaceful terms we'll all live happily ever after."

The confused hobo decided he might be safer back at the shelter.

"We know how to be generous." Mr. Perkins went on. "And in time to insure a lasting peace we'll even provide imported acorn pate from France." The hobo stumbled and fell backwards onto a bench. He looked at Mr. Perkins and scratched his head. "Otherwise, I fear the Neighborhood Watch will take drastic actions to eliminate your entire species. They're on the brink of war."

Frightened, the hobo managed to climb to his feet.

"As soon as my colleagues appear you'll have the finest bottled water. But you must promise to call off your brethren that we may resolve our differences."

"Mr. Perkins, Mr. Perkins," Eleanor and Maize called, "we've got the water."

With a cry, the hobo lurched off the bench and fled.

"Who was that?" Eleanor asked. She handed Mr. Perkins a large bottle of expensive water. "We made wishes for her to appear," she said.

"In the wishing well at Mall Mart," Maize said.

"Really," Mr. Perkins said. "Well that certainly explains…" His jaw dropped as a huge, filmy, squirrel-shaped being appeared before them.

Eleanor dropped to her knees. Maize gazed open mouthed.

The wavering image solidified and there stood a combination of squirrel and person, with a human face and hands, large furry wings and a lovely fluffy tail.

Eleanor recovered first. She stood and held out her clasped hands. "Please ask the red squirrels to stop their mischief," she said. "Homeowners are on the brink of war. They want to use poisonous chemicals."

"We'll bring you water every week," Maize put in reverently. "Any kind you like."

Mr. Perkins held out the bottled water.

The Deva's wings fluttered. Her human hands reached out and took the fancy bottle. She smiled, nodded and disappeared.

When Mr. Perkins returned home, the red squirrels were cavorting happily in his garden and not a single plant had been disturbed.

The Little Footstool

Moving day was soon approaching. Having decided to downsize, the couple that lived in the white house up the street had recently bought a smaller one just down the road. This meant that they had to choose very carefully what they would keep and bring with them versus what they would pass on.

The lady of the house preferred comfortable and useful furniture. She was, however, sentimental about a few old family pieces she remembered from her girlhood visits to her grandmother's house in Boston: The Federalist highboy with its many drawers and polished brass handles, the scuffed up old pine desk said by members of her family to have been used by none other than George Washington himself when he had visited Boston during the early days of the Revolution, and the old, battered footstool, now tattered and, in her husband's opinion, looking a little too worse for wear.

Her husband had little interest in furniture and, like his wife, preferred comfort to style. He did, however, carry on the family tradition: telling grandchildren and visitors alike how the rare antique pine desk was used by General Washington to write significant messages to Lafayette that no doubt turned the tide of the Revolution in favor of the colonists.

Neither the wife nor her husband had any idea that, in the wee small hours when they were fast asleep, the furniture talked amongst themselves in a language known only to them.

"I know I'll be going to the new house," the teak coffee table said confidently. "After all, I'm a table, and for as long as human history can remember, people have always put things on their tables."

"I'm sure to be going along as well," the bentwood rocker told the floor lamp. "She always sits on me when she reads her mail. Nothing like us Bentwoods for world class rest and relaxation."

"No doubt we'll be the first in the new home," the rare colonial pine desk told the Federalist highboy. "After all, without us, fair's to say they'd look like everyone else—no class at all!"

"True," agreed the highboy. "Of course, should there be a space consideration, I might be donated to one of the better museums. Decent tax write-offs that way." The highboy beamed, envisioning itself in a room full of Chippendales and rare, beautifully-polished grandfather clocks.

"She'll certainly take us along," the two standing floor lamps chorused. "Sound wiring, bright three-way light. I'd say we have nothing to be concerned over. You, on the other hand," the taller of the two lamps said down to the footstool. "If anything around here is thrift shop bound, it's you."

The little footstool with the stubby legs felt sad. It had enjoyed its time in the white house, especially when the lady of the house would sing while watering her plants. It even remembered her as a girl, sitting in one of her grandmother's Martha Washington chairs kicking her shoes against its sides.

"And if you're too tattered for the thrift shop and winter's as cold as they say it will be, well then there's always kindling," bullied the old pine desk.

"Footstools have become so passé," the teak coffee table sneered." In today's world it's beanbag chairs and sectional sofas facing the TV that dress up a room. Personally I doubt you'll stand a chance of ever going to the new house."

These rude remarks saddened the little footstool. It took pride in its stuffed embroidered cover set upon a sturdy wooden frame, and especially its neat little claw footed feet. The embroidery might be a wee bit tattered, but over the years, despite its stubby, fat little legs, the little footstool had always considered itself a treasure with classic charm.

"Hear tell they're going to have a yard sale before the final move," the highboy told the pine desk. "Clean out the riffraff, you know." The little footstool felt sure that that last remark was intended for it to hear.

Over the next few days the husband and wife walked around the house making long lists of what furniture they thought they'd take with them versus what they thought they'd leave behind. Each list differed from the previous one until finally, throwing her arms up in frustrated desperation, the wife announced that night at supper to her husband that she had called up Maggie Thrash, President of the local Historical Society and past President of the celebrated Colonial Furniture League, to stop by for tea and render her esteemed opinion as to what might best be kept versus what could be moved on.

"I can see how people get addicted to furniture," the husband commented. "Personally, I wish we could just go buy everything new and have that up-scale *Architectural Digest* look."

"We'd have to spend a fortune," his wife said practically. "Let's just let Maggie decide. She has an eye for good taste."

"I suppose if it doesn't fit upstairs we could always put the highboy in the basement," the husband commented. "It would make an ideal container for all my tools."

"Basement!" cried the highboy in alarm, breaking a cardinal rule of not speaking in the presence of people. "Tools! That's the last thing I want to have happen."

"Did you hear something," asked the husband?

"Must be the wind," the wife said, gazing fondly at the small, tattered footstool she felt so drawn to despite its obvious shabbiness.

"It's just talk," the colonial desk whispered to the highboy. "Pay no attention to anything they say. Without the two of us, they're strictly déclassé."

A few days later Maggie Thrash came for a visit. She paid little if any attention to the lamps, the Bentwood rocker or the teak coffee table. Much to its dismay, she looked suspiciously at the old pine desk.

"Are you sure this is the real McCoy?" she asked the wife, her gnarled fingers stroking the wood.

"My grandmother always called it George Washington's desk," the wife smiled.

But Maggie shook her head. "Something about it. I'm not sure what. But something screams replica."

"Really," said the wife. "Are you sure?"

Something about the way the wood is bonded. Could be a very slick reproduction from the 1920's.

"What do you think about the highboy?" the

husband asked. "I've always thought it was a handsome piece."

Hearing this, the highboy drew itself up proudly and waited to hear more. Maggie looked it over carefully, her lips curling a bit. "Hmmm, hard to say. True, it's old," she paused searching for the right words. "But, well, it's a common piece, nothing very special. It will certainly do to keep your tools in, however. You'll find it useful I'm sure. Say now." She put down her teacup, stood up and went over to the little footstool. "What have we here?"

"It's been in my family for years," smiled the wife, "a bit tattered I'm afraid, but I couldn't bear to part with it."

"Yes, and it's mahogany," Maggie Thrash said excitedly I'd dare say it's worth more than anything else in this house. Way, Queen Victoria might have rested her tiny feet upon it. I'll offer you six thousand dollars for it, right now," she licked her lips impatiently.

"Oh, no, I would never part with it," said the wife, picking it up and hugging it to her. "I love it dearly."

"Well then, I'm going to suggest that our Historical Society borrow it and place it in a prominent place in our forthcoming décor display."

"You old fool," the pine desk burst out "I'm not a replica. I'm not. I'm not."

"You know nothing about vintage American furnishings," screeched the highboy.

All three of the humans stopped speaking and listened. "Someone say something?" Maggie frowned."

"I think it's the wind," the wife said. "It's been so windy lately."

"I've always loved that little footstool of yours too," smiled her husband. "Maybe it's just what we need to dress up the new house.

"I believe you're right," said his wife. "And of course, Queen Victoria or not, we'll have it carefully restored."

That night, the highboy and the old pine desk commiserated with one another. "What does she know?" they continually murmured.

In the darkness, the little footstool sang happily to itself, "I always knew I was special," it said, "and best of all, she loves me."

Comedians' Lunch

Sitting at a table in Heaven's bustling Celebrity Bistro, George Burns twirled an anchovy on a toothpick. Across from him Gracie Allen looked up from reading *Variety*. "Always showing off, George."

At a nearby table, Milton Berle giggled as several Ziegfeld Folly girls ran their fingers through his toupée. "Don't let my mother see you doing that. She paid a lot for this rug."

"And it's not even an Oriental." George Jessel cracked. "Next thing you know you'll be charging for autographed photos just like Benny does."

"I heard that!" Jack Benny snapped. He beckoned to his waiter and handed him a heavy shopping bag.

The angelic waiter looked nonplussed. "What's this Mr. Benny?"

"Green stamps to pay for my lunch," Jack said. "Rochester can pick up his own tab."

"We're in Heaven, Mr. Benny, where everyone's expected to be generous," Rochester said. "Jesus might have saved a lot, but once Moses started investing around here money grew on trees."

"Never have I seen such an expensive menu," Jack complained. "What does God do with all that money anyway? Send His angels to college?" He looked at the waiter. "And if there's not enough in there," he brandished his violin case, "I can always play a little

Paganini."

"Keep your Paganini to yourself," Jessel snapped. "I want to enjoy my lunch in peace."

Jimmy Durante breezed into the cafeteria. "You've got to start off each day with a smile…" He grinned at Gracie. "How about a little gin this afternoon, Doll Face?"

Gracie smiled. "Oh Jimmy, I'd rather drink Champagne."

"How can you afford to eat here, Durante?" Jack Benny asked. "Forty five dollars for a corned beef sandwich with fries and a side of slaw is outrageous!"

"Mrs. Calabash left me a lot more than her husband's pipe collection," Durante quipped.

Gracie looked up from *Variety*. "Listen to this, George: Madonna's looking for a new male lead for her upcoming movie. Why not get reborn and go audition?"

George shook his head.

"Why not?" Gracie asked. "You always said you wanted a role with Madonna or Sharon Stone. Now's your chance."

"And Gracie can stay with me and Mary," Jack Benny added. "We've lovely rooms with an ultra-modern kitchen so she can do the cooking. Plus we'll charge her less rent than anyone else would."

George puffed on his cigar. "Because I'm Jewish, Gracie. And when you're Jewish you only get born once every thousand years."

"So become something else, George. Like maybe a Libertarian, or even a Vegetarian."

"Shouldn't matter what you become," Jessel cracked.

"Haven't you heard? If you go back far enough, everybody's Jewish."

"If anybody around here should get reborn, it's me," Jimmy Durante quipped. "Why, I can sing and dance, and even keep everyone in stitches."

"Whether they have health insurance or not," Jessel said.

"Maybe I should get reborn," Milton Berle said. "Why, I've played the Palace more times than the Queen."

"Which queen is that?" George Burns asked.

"There's only one thing worse than not working," Milton lamented. "And that's being forgotten."

"Oh, Uncle Milty, we're not forgotten," Gracie said. "It's just that people don't remember us anymore."

"Gracie," George asked, "who are those two guys in suits of armor keeping an eye on you?"

Gracie smiled. "Oh, that's Sir Galahad and Sir Lancelot. We met before you got here, George." She waved to them. They smiled back. "George, give Lancelot a cigar."

"Why should I? You know I hate giving away my cigars. How did you happen to meet them, anyway?"

"Well as soon as I checked in, St. Peter told me I needed an escort. By the way, George, what took you so long?" She sniffed. "You once said you could never live without me."

George puffed on his cigar. "That was before I played God, Gracie."

"No wonder!" Gracie sighed. "My Uncle Nestor played God, but mostly at holidays around the

Christmas tree."

"Gave nice gifts?" George asked.

"No," Gracie frowned. "He always thought his presence was enough."

"You played God!?" Jack Benny's voice rose. "So that's why it's so expensive around here! Come on Rochester, let's go get burgers and fries at the fast food restaurant."

"So long as they're not deep fried, Mr. Benny." Rochester cautioned. "You know where you've got to go to get deep fried!" He rolled his eyes and pointed downward.

"Actually, Gracie, after having played God in three movies, I'd like to say hello and see if He liked how I portrayed Him."

"Oh, you can schedule an appointment with Him anytime, George. He holds regular office hours just like a dentist or a chiropodist. But I'm sure He's much too busy to go to the movies."

"From what I've heard," Durante said, "there's a long line, and you'll have to wait ten thousand years for an appointment with Him."

George raised his eyebrows. "Ten thousand years to talk to God! Why should it take that long?"

"So He can devote his attention to taking care of the living, George," Gracie replied.

George tapped his cigar into an ashtray that an angel promptly emptied. "How's that, Gracie?"

"He wants to be sure people continue to believe in Him. Do you have any idea how many times a day someone yells, 'Oh God' this, or 'Oh God' that?"

As the angelic wait-staff prepared for the evening meal, only a few diners lingered on at the Heavenly Bistro. George Burns looked up from the remnants of his crab-meat roll. "Gracie, I still can't believe one has to wait ten thousand years for an audience with God. Why, I could be reincarnated over and over before I'd have a chance to meet Him."

"That's the whole idea, George. That's why He and Confucius invented the wheel."

"So people wouldn't get confused."

"Something like that."

"But couldn't I be an exception? After all, back in vaudeville I was a famous song-and-dance man. Plus I did play Him in the movies."

"There's only one person who can see Him whenever he wants."

"Who? A famous Rabbi or Pope?"

"No! Charlton Heston. He's played so many Biblical roles that now he gets special privileges."

"How did you find all this out? I thought you said it took ten thousand years to get an appointment."

"It does to see Him, but not to see Her. She's usually available."

George shook his head. "I don't understand."

Gracie set down the remains of her tuna melt. "You see, George, God has both a male and a female side. And I happen to be friends with His female side."

"How's that, Gracie?"

"Oh, we meet at the beauty parlor."

"You mean God gets Her hair done just like everybody else? What color does She use?"

"Only her hairdresser knows for sure, George. All I can tell you is that we both really like a good hot cup of coffee."

"But if the He side is so busy, then what does the She side do all day?"

"Oh, you know, just like any other woman; raises her kids, keeps her home clean and tidy, does a lot of cooking; and to keep up with the times She even went back to school and got an advanced degree in marketing."

George looked nonplussed. "You mean She writes ads?"

"I think it's more like letting people know what He's got on His plate. That way everyone knows what's going on."

George nodded astutely. "Tell me, Gracie, how did you get so settled here without having me around to help you out?"

"Being in Heaven's just like being in the movies. The first thing you do is to go to Wardrobe. They have this wonderful beautician there who can help you look any age as long as it's young. And the clothes, George, you wouldn't believe the choices."

"You seem to really know your way around, Gracie. Who are some of your friends?"

"Oh, most of them were in show biz like us. But I do know Myron Schultz and Beethoven."

George beamed. "Do you think I could ever meet Beethoven? I certainly love his Fifth!"

Gracie paused. "I didn't know he ever drank. He

seemed so sober those times when we talked."

"That's his Fifth Symphony, Gracie." George waved his finger like a baton. "You know, Dum de de dum! Dum de de dum! Dum dum dum dum dum dum dum dum…"

Gracie frowned. "Personally, George, if I were you I wouldn't go calling Beethoven dumb. That sounds very disrespectful."

"No, Gracie. I was just humming the opening measure to his Fifth Symphony."

"Well I think it's rude to call his Symphony dumb too. He couldn't help it if he was underprivileged. The poor guy went deaf, and back then they didn't have good hearing aids."

"I really wasn't."

She shrugged and picked up her copy of *Variety*. "Listen to this! Groucho Marx is hosting a special Christmas party tonight and all comedians are invited."

Milton Berle paused as he passed their table. He leaned over and peered at *Variety*. "I hear Groucho's got all the waitresses dressed like Vegas showgirls." He snickered. "It's going to be some party."

George cleared his throat. "Gracie, not to change the subject, but who's that rumpled dour person over there staring at you? That isn't Beethoven, is it?"

Gracie giggled. "No, George, that's Fred Allen." She waved and called out, "Hi Fred!"

"Gracie!" Fred joined them. "Hi Milton, see you at Groucho's. Oh, George, I didn't see you."

"Hello, Fred. What are you doing here?"

"Just waiting till it's time for Groucho's party. Should

be fun and if you say the secret word you'll win a hundred dollars. Plus as a special treat he's got George Fenneman arm-wrestling Ed McMahon."

Fred peered at the crusts of Gracie's tuna melt. "If you're not going to finish that... The prices on the menu are out of this world."

George smiled. "That's exactly what Jack Benny said."

Fred looked aghast. "You mean me and Benny finally agree on something?"

"You bet your life," George said.

Gracie sniffed. "I wouldn't go that far George. What if you lost?"

"In Heaven, you can't lose."

"That's all right, then."

George stood up and helped Gracie from her chair. "It's time to get ready for Groucho's party. Say 'Merry Christmas' and 'Happy New Year', Gracie. Oh, one last thing, who's Myron Schultz? Is he a producer I don't know?"

Gracie smiled her wonderful smile. "No, he was my mother's butcher in Hoboken, and he always had the best brisket. Merry Christmas and Happy New Year, everybody. See you all next year."

The Girl of His Dreams

The on-line ad promised him the girl of your dreams. *What could be better than that*, Tim thought.

Divorced, living alone, nearly forty, slightly overweight and out of shape, Tim was not into the singles dating scene. He'd been hopeful of finding his dream girl ever since his ex had walked out on him three years ago, but until now he had no idea how to make that happen.

He clicked on the ad and spent the next several hours filling in comprehensive forms.

He was asked about his dating preferences from adolescence to the present. Then he answered several hundred intimate questions about himself, his expectations, and what in a woman would make him happy. Exhausted, he finished the forms, punched in his credit card data, and went to bed.

On a Saturday afternoon six weeks later, his doorbell rang. He had just finished lunch and was about to turn on a Red Sox game.

Standing there was an attractive blond of perhaps thirty five with sparkling blue eyes and an infectious smile. She wore a dark tailored power suit, boots with heels and she carried a raincoat over her shoulder. She had a small attaché case as well as her purse.

"Hello, Tim," she smiled. "I'm Judith, from The Girl of Your Dreams Inc. But please, just call me Judy."

He gulped. Drop-dead gorgeous, she looked like one of the movie stars at the Academy Awards.

"Hi Judy. Come on in."

Her beauty overwhelmed him and he was wordless. How odd, he'd always thought of himself as an extrovert—outgoing, out of the box, a phrase maker as they called him at the ad agency where he worked.

He gestured for her to join him. "H-h-how lovely you are," he heard himself stammer as he led her into his condo. "This is unbelievable. It's h-h-hard to believe something like this could really be happening."

She laughed and winked at him. "Oh, it's happening all right, and aren't you glad? I must say I am." Her voice softened. "You're such a handsome man." She put her hand on his arm. "Aren't I the lucky one?"

He gulped. He'd never been called handsome. "I'm just me," he said.

Judy went to the picture window overlooking the Charles. "What a super view. Is that where you walk? Strolling along the river with you will be so romantic." She fluttered her eyelids.

Tim smiled shyly. "Are you flirting with me?"

She smiled again. "I'm just me," she echoed. She linked her arm in his. "I so look forward to our getting to know each other. Show me around your condo, won't you please?"

She looked around; her eyes lit up. "Oh, Tim, if you'd like we can repaint it, in your favorite colors of course. I'm happy to do the painting. And I can sew new drapes and slip covers if you'd like to brighten up the look." She nodded at him confidently. "I have many useful talents, just as you requested when you filled out the forms."

"I kind of like my place the way it is." He remembered checking off talented and confident, but this was amazing.

"Why don't I fix you a meal? Tell me what you like to eat. I'm trained in gourmet cooking and I'll make sure that whatever I make will be completely healthy as well as enjoyable."

"Err, I just ate. And besides, I... I don't have much on hand. Why don't we go out for dinner, eventually?"

"Oh, but I could make you a gourmet meal out of whatever you have in your cupboard."

As they went into the bedroom, she opened the door to his closet and ran her hands over his suits. "I'm also an experienced seamstress. I'll happily refurbish your entire wardrobe, a stitch here, a stitch there, and you'll be a fashion plate."

"What's wrong with my clothes?" He began rubbing the back of his neck. "And I like eating out. Besides, there's nothing in the fridge but frozen peas and orange juice." Was this really the girl of his dreams?

"I remember on the form you said you like to be read to at night." She opened her attaché case and held out a copy of *Treasure Island*. "Isn't this one of your favorites?"

He didn't know quite what to say. Finally he stammered, "It's still sunny out. Let's go for a walk along the Charles."

As they walked down Beacon Street, two men in hoodies and masks jumped in front of them. One, brandishing a large knife, grabbed Judy. She delivered a series of karate chops. In desperation the muggers fled.

She dusted off her hands, smiled and took his arm. "There, now all's well."

Tim looked at her and sighed. She might be the girl of his dreams, but what did she need him for? He shook his head.

She looked into his eyes. "I've been manufactured to your exact specifications by my company, and I promise I'll fulfill your every expectation. You see, Tim, I'm everything you said you wanted me to be. Tell me, sir, does that please you?"

Abracadabra Moonshine

Blast the Wonder Pig, golden brown with a bright white star in the middle of his forehead, walked through the back door of Zeke's cabin. He trudged over and put his trotters up on the long table where Zeke was hammering out a silver and turquoise bracelet.

Suddenly, in his mind, Zeke saw a snapshot of his ex wife, Maga, taken years ago when they were newlyweds. "Maga!" he said aloud. "Think she'll call?"

Blast nodded his head and grunted.

"That bad, huh?" Zeke got up and took a can of beer from the fridge. "What's she gotten herself into this time?"

Blast closed his eyes and lowered his head.

Zeke's eyes widened. In his mind he saw an image of an older, heavier Maga, her hair still long and wavy but streaked with gray. She wore a peasant blouse and jeans. As he watched, she handed someone one of the wallets he had made thirty years ago.

Blast turned his attention to his cooler in the pantry Zeke kept it stocked with gourmet cheeses. He selected one flavored with truffles and retired to enjoy it.

Together they shared Zeke's cabin in the desert hours south of Tucson. Its one big room was a chaos of clutter. Books were stacked between cans of chili and old magazines. Bags of soybeans and assorted dry foods leaned between boxes of silver and assorted gemstones.

Blast and Zeke lived comfortably in the space between the long table, Zeke's futon couch, bookcases, a rocker facing a big TV, and Blast's hay-filled bed.

Out of nowhere, six years ago, Blast had appeared at Zeke's cabin door. When Zeke opened it, he and Blast instantly bonded. As they eyed each other, Zeke knew that here was some very special bacon materialized by divine intervention. In his head he heard the name Blast. "Blast the Wonder Pig, that's who you are!" Now they were good buddies.

"I guess some ex-wives from back then hold on no matter how many other husbands they've had," Zeke said.

Blast nodded and lapped water.

"Back then" was UCLA in 1974, where Zeke had been an enthusiastic psychology professor. Even today his best selling pop-psych classic, *Nothing Doing,* still paid him a decent royalty.

He'd seen Maga in the audience at one of his lectures. They made eye contact and flirted. Afterward they dined and by morning had become an item. Back then Maga taught dance with an experimental theater company in LA, wrote romantic potboilers under a pseudonym, and labored over finishing her thesis on elves. Their marriage had lasted close to twelve years before they had called it quits.

Zeke knew that today Maga still wrote potboilers, was a High Priestess in an urban coven, and still dabbled in charm craft. Only now she lived on the East Coast near Boston.

When they broke up, Zeke left LA. He told friends he'd be taking a walkabout. He assured everyone that he'd be back, but that never happened. In the desert

Zeke's search for his ultimate nothingness had led him to discover ancient Indian ruins that contained the lost secrets of Abracadabra Moonshine.

His phone rang. Blast yawned.

"Zeke!" It was Maga's voice. "I know it's late, but I need your help. And please don't get angry. I promise I'll never do anything like this again."

"What?" He couldn't help but wonder if she had put on as much weight as he had.

Her voice slid down several octaves. "It was a very innocuous charm."

Zeke swore. "You know better than to go mess like that!"

"I need to straighten things out and get them back to the way they were. Nothing else."

He yawned. "Go on."

"Remember those leather wallets you made that we charmed?"

"Yes."

"Well, it worked, honey. I gifted one to someone I just knew really needed a new wallet. His name is Henry Perkins."

Zeke felt impatient. "And?"

"The next week, he brings it back and tells me it's defective. He said every time he takes out a dollar what comes out is a hundred."

Zeke laughed. "Nothing wrong with that!"

"Well, to him there is. Henry's a retired accountant and takes money very seriously."

"This guy sounds like a real a piece of work."

"I offered to exchange it, but he said how much he

liked the way it fit in his pocket, and would I just fix it. I
thought I could unravel the charm we had put into that
batch of leather."

"Go on."

Her voice dropped. "It gets worse."

Blast yawned and snorted.

"He thought that the bills might be counterfeit or
tied into an IRS sting operation. I knew I had to help
him. Plus I think he's sweet. So I did a banishing and
asked that no more hundreds come out. Period. And
none do. Instead, Confederate banknotes pour out like a
fountain every time he opens it."

Blast sat up and grunted. Zeke swore. "And there's
more, isn't there?"

"Yes!" She sighed. "When he looks at people, he sees
gigantic insects, wild birds, or half-human creatures.
This is very disconcerting for him. Imagine how you'd
feel stopping at a diner for breakfast and seeing a row
of vultures on the stools along the counter drinking
coffee?"

Even after all these years, Zeke's volatility riled
Maga's nerves. Against her better judgment, to calm
down, she lit a cigarette and took small, delicate puffs.
"Zeke, please listen. I'm trying to help this man. He's a
widower. I feel sorry for him. He doesn't deserve this."

Zeke shouted. "You have no idea what you've done!"

Maga raised her voice. "I told you, I'm trying to help
him. Please help me."

He snapped. "Why should I?"

Blast turned and walked toward to his cooler.

Maga screeched. "Listen, Zeke, we pulled this little

stunt together. We're in it up to our eyeballs. Don't think you're not!"

"I had nothing to do with this," he grumbled.

"Nevertheless, if this was ever brought before the magical community, you'd be branded an undesirable and shunned in any reputable circles."

He took a deep breath. He could care less about her and her reputable circles. What did matter, however, was staying in balance with the universe.

Zeke lowered his voice. "What you did with that wallet inadvertently opened astral portals. Energies from the past leaked into the present and are challenging reality. People may start seeing things that aren't there. But things could get way worse."

"How?"

"Reality could come completely apart."

She shuddered. "That's horrible."

"I know. Get the wallet back. How many others have you sold?"

"I just started selling them. I found them at the bottom of a trunk. You had made thirty and twenty-three are left.

"Hang onto them. Don't sell anymore. Did anyone else complain or say anything?"

"No! Would you?"

Zeke chuckled. "There's no telling where something like this could lead to. It's not just cut-and-dried and made for American TV."

She sighed and stubbed out the cigarette. Her voice softened. "Yes dear, I know. And Zeke, thanks for helping me. And I'm sorry I got upset."

Blast yawned, climbed off his bed, looked at Zeke and then at the big TV. It was time for his favorite show, *Animal Planet*.

Zeke turned it on. "Just get that wallet back, and I'll burn it along with all the rest."

She knew better than to argue. "One last thing." Her tone of voice changed: "If need be, could you come and help me?"

Zeke's face reddened. "Now you're asking a lot. I'll have to check with Blast."

She looked quizzical. "Blast! Who's Blast?"

"My partner. He's a pig. We live together."

"Really!" She sounded surprised. "Now that's different for you, isn't it?"

"You could say that," Zeke said. "He's a real shape-shifting pig. I've never met anyone quite like him before." He ended the call and finished his beer.

When *Animal Planet* ended, Zeke and Blast had a council of war. Afterward, Blast climbed onto his bed and Zeke and went to the cabinet. Carefully, he removed his ancient magical stones and set them out on his long table.

Then he sat and meditated. The light of Abracadabra Moonshine flowed through him.

The next morning, Mr. Perkins had just finished breakfast when a car pulled into his driveway. He peered out the window and momentarily recoiled when a curvaceous Persian cat in high heels with a trim white-leather sack slung over her shoulder emerged from the driver's side.

"Not again!" Mr. Perkins lamented. "Will these nightmares never end?" The doorbell rang.

Maga did not expect to see a youthful, boyish Henry Perkins. He looked barely out of school. But she knew that couldn't true. How could it? "Hello... Henry?"

"That's me," his voice squeaked.

"Really! You seem so young. Don't you recognize me? It's me, Maga from the Senior Center craft show."

"Well, yes," Mr. Perkins said tactfully. "I just wasn't sure, but now that you've mentioned it... Do come in and sit down."

She looked at him oddly. "Are you all right? I must talk to you. It's very important."

"Oh, I'm fine."

"Then why don't you look like you should instead of like an adolescent?"

"Why do you look like a Persian cat?" Mr. Perkins countered.

"I do? That's surprising. No one ever put it quite that way before."

She sat at his kitchen table. He poured them both some coffee. "To what do I owe this visit?"

Her voice quivered. She tried to smile. "I've come for the wallet, Henry. I must have it back so that it can be fixed. Then I'll return it to you."

"You really think I look younger? May I take that as a compliment?"

Before Maga could reply, a large golden brown pig with a white star in the middle of its forehead appeared.

Mr. Perkins smiled and said. "Oh, hello. Are you

another friend of Maga's? Do join us. May I pour you a cup of coffee?"

"Henry, that's a real pig." Maga stammered.

"Yes," Mr. Perkins smiled. "And you're a Persian cat. Shall I fix us all some lunch? How about tuna fish sandwiches?"

"But Henry, that's a real pig."

Blast didn't help matters then when, just after Henry went upstairs to get the wallet, he shape-shifted into the actor Humphrey Bogart looking as he appeared in *Casablanca*.

Moments later, Henry rushed into the kitchen clutching a raft of Confederate bills. "The wallet's gone. These were all that was in my bureau drawer."

Bogie grinned at Maga. "Here's looking at you, kid." Then he vanished.

Maga sat at Mr. Perkins' kitchen table. She forced herself to take five long, connected breaths. Then she looked at the youthful Henry Perkins.

"Did Humphrey Bogart just walk through here?"

"I didn't see him. Just you and a pig wearing a trench coat and fedora."

"You didn't see him turn into Humphrey Bogart? He wore the exact same trench coat he wore in *Casablanca*."

Mr. Perkins smiled. He wondered how close this Persian cat was to losing her mind, but tactfully asked, "And why would he do that?"

She said with finality, "I think he took your wallet and disappeared with it."

"What should we do?" Mr. Perkins pulled at his hair. He'd never been robbed before. "Call the police. Report a robbery. Say a wallet was stolen. That would certainly bring a squad car."

"I wouldn't!" Maga said. "What would you say? That Humphrey Bogart stole your wallet?"

"No," Mr. Perkins said emphatically. "I'd say a pig made off with it."

Maga looked at this innocent boy of a man. She wanted to take him home and teach him the ways of the world. Then she realized what she was thinking and gulped. "Once word got out, don't you think saying something that unbelievable might create a poor opinion of you?"

"Before all this happened I'd certainly have agreed with you," Mr. Perkins said. "And," he smiled, "whatever else you look like, you are a handsome Persian cat. I might have to buy one as a house pet after all this is over."

"Oh, Henry, I'm so sorry to have accidentally put you through all this. You are such a kind, caring and understanding man."

Mr. Perkins patted her paw and stroked her back. He was glad she was a Persian cat. When he stroked her back, her coat would positively ripple.

An unexpected flash of energy exploded and caught Maga's attention by storm. She blinked and lost track of what they were talking about. She heard herself start to purr.

"But now," Mr. Perkins nodded, "I realize there's so much more to life than I've ever thought possible. How else can I explain a pig walking in here and taking that wallet? I'm sure if I tell my story as it happened, others who have the same kinds of experiences might feel better about themselves. Yes, I feel it right for me to do this."

Maga's head was spinning. She decided to take another tack. "Henry, please understand that, within magic circles, there is a very important code of silence."

Mr. Perkins wrinkled his brow.

Her voice softened to practically a whisper. "You must never speak of this. You have no idea of the repercussions that could occur. You could well start a war between realities."

He lowered his eyes. He didn't believe a word she was saying. "What does reality have to do with this?"

Maga finished her coffee. "At the very least, you'd be declared a lunatic and locked up for the rest of your life. People who see what you can see are considered a threat to those who cannot."

"I never really gave anything like that much thought. This isn't the Middle Ages, you know. People don't get locked away when they say it rains frogs. And that's a proven fact." He chuckled and was glad he remembered recently reading about that in a magazine.

Maga stretched luxuriously. Ripples of energy moved through her. Her eyes lit up. "How about our getting away from here for a little while, just the two of us, someplace where we can relax and talk more."

He considered that.

"Strange things seem to be happening in your house."

"That's very true."

"I have a guest room in my garden apartment. You

could really relax, feel peaceful and at one with yourself. I'll fix whatever you like for dinner." She smiled. Mr. Perkins heard her purr.

He nodded. He'd never been invited anywhere by a Persian cat, especially by one who offered to do the cooking. "Yes," he smiled. "A rest. That's exactly what I need; peace and quiet away from here. I'll lock up and let's go."

If more men saw their wives as cats, she thought, *there'd be a lot more happy marriages in the world.*

When Zeke came back from the library, he saw Mr. Perkins' wallet on the long table. He looked at Blast. "You met Maga?"

Blast hooted and moved his head up and down.

"That good still!" Zeke laughed.

Blast nodded and came closer to the long table.

As Zeke opened the wallet it jumped from his hands. Confederate banknotes flooded out. By the time he pushed it shut there were enough to wallpaper a small room.

Blast made what sounded like a series of belching hiccups as he peered at the money.

"You're right," Zeke said. "Might be a good idea if you went back and got the rest of them. No telling where she keeps the stuff she sells.

Blast sniffed the wallet.

Mr. Perkins was impressed with Maga's apartment. Plants shaded the windows and long flowering vines crawled along the tops of bookcases. There was a comfortable, white down sectional. Two palm trees in large bright orange pots shaded a kidney shaped coffee table cluttered with books.

Maga still looked like a Persian cat and that worried Mr. Perkins. Seeing people as creatures or mythic beasts seemed to be becoming more frequent. Still, he assured himself that this was just bad luck and that he wasn't losing his mind.

"I heard you thinking." She pranced in from her kitchen holding a small tray of crackers and cheese in her forepaws. "I thought we'd have a little snack."

"Yes. Thank you." He smiled. "With all this excitement I forget to eat."

"I do that all the time," she purred. "Maybe we could remind each other."

He nodded and smiled. "I like the way you think."

"Really," Maga smiled and felt overcome by his charm. "Dare I pour us each a glass of sherry?"

His eyes glazed. "Helen loved sherry at this time in the afternoon."

Maga nodded, remembering he had mentioned Helen before. She fought off the urge to clutch him in her arms. She found that strange considering he was far from the fantasy he-man type she'd think about when the moon was full.

"I'm glad it's OK with my seeing you as a big fluffy Persian cat. I'm sure other women might get upset."

She handed him his glass and sat close to him on the couch.

Henry sighed. "But I must say it's difficult always seeing you as a cat."

She purred against his shoulder. "I should think it

would be."

He smiled. "But I'm getting the hang of seeing people as creatures. Now, when I see someone who looks like he's out of *Ripley's Believe It Or Not,* I tell myself it's OK and I'm not going crazy."

She cuddled closer to him. "Oh, Henry, don't think about crazy. It's such an overblown word. You're just tuned into an alternate reality."

"I am? Now that's a new thought." He sipped some sherry and took a slice of cheese.

She purred. "How else am I like Helen?"

"Her thinking was as unexplainable as her actions—she never used a recipe. She only cooked from her own mind. You could call her an original thinker, like you." He smiled as he remembered Helen's apple pie.

"Yes," Maga nodded and patted his cheek. "Please excuse me while I go slip into something a little more comfortable?"

Rising, she waved at a wall of books and a cabinet of bric-a-brac. "Please, make yourself at home. You might find something fun to read or look at, but if not you might find my little succulent garden by the window interesting." She blew him a kiss and pranced toward her bedroom waving her beautiful long, white tail.

Maga gasped as she opened her bedroom door.

"Where's the rest of the wallets, sweetheart?" Bogie tilted his fedora.

She closed the door, "Whoever you are you have no right breaking into my room."

"Nothing broken, sweetheart. Not one speck of dust out of place."

"Who are you? Are you tied in with Zeke?"

"Just hand over the wallets. No time for small talk."

"First you come clean with me and tell me who you are. Be real."

To answer her query, Blast appeared momentarily in his natural pig skin, then shape-shifted back into the living persona of Bogie.

Maga was nonplused. "I've never seen anything like you in my life." She leaned against her bureau, calm but watchful. "If Zeke sent you for the wallets, tell him he can have them. I'll give them to you tomorrow morning. But they're not here. They're in my locker at the Senior Center. Now will you please go away? I'm entertaining a guest."

"Not so fast," Bogie said. "Let's you and me go for a ride."

"No one will be there. They'll be closed; the building will be locked. We can go in the morning as soon as they open."

There was a loud crash. Maga eyes widened. She pulled opened her bedroom door and rushed down the hall to the living room. Her collection of succulents had swelled their way out of their pots. Broken pottery littered the floor.

"Henry, are you all right?"

"Yes, but I fear being around me has caused your plants to grow like they're on steroids. It's part of what's happening to me," Mr. Perkins sighed. "Helen's begonia did the same, grew disproportionately. I had to put it outside. I wish that whatever this it is would stop. I can't stand it anymore. I need to get away."

"Yes," she agreed swirling her tail. "I'll take you

away."

Bogie appeared in the doorway. "Not so fast, sister."

But Mr. Perkins didn't see Blast's Bogie façade. Indignantly, he said, "You're the pig who broke into my house. You may well be a talking pig, but you're still a criminal, and I've a good mind to report you to the police."

"It's alright, Henry," Maga said softly. "He's only here to get the rest of the wallets." She slunk over to him. "Zeke sent him. He's a magical being that's probably a whole lot more powerful than Zeke is."

The negative effects of the wallets were getting worse. From the back seat of Maga's car as Blast drove them to the Senior Center, Mr. Perkins saw rhinos, hippos, and giraffes carrying handbags and tromping in and out of stores. Outside Mall Mart, brazen cougars in startling bikinis handed out free samples of cosmetics. Wolves appeared to be directing traffic; pigeons in high heels crowded the sidewalks.

"I just have to accept that for the rest of my life I'll be living in a human zoo," he said. "I never knew things like this could happen."

"You're seeing people in some sort of alternate reality. But it won't last forever," Maga purred.

"I suppose," he said. "But until it changes, Saturday's church supper could be challenging. Right now, I accept that I'm here in a car being driven by a pig, and sitting next to him is a Persian cat. "

"Yes, Henry," Maga smiled. "You're being very brave."

She pointed at Blast. "He's a shape-shifter. They straddle alternate realities. They can do lots of things we can't."

Bogie wheeled into the Senior Center lot and parked. Maga looked shocked. "You're really determined we go in there now, aren't you?"

Bogie grinned. "That's how it looks to me, sweetheart." He jingled a thick brass key ring. "Should be simple."

He and Maga climbed out. Blast jerked his trotter at Mr. Perkins indicating he come along. Maga helped him out of the back seat and slid her paw into his hand. "I'm sorry, Henry. I hope this experience with a shape-shifter doesn't prejudice your thinking about magic in general."

"I'm certainly not that close-minded. But please, tell me where these alternate realities are so I can be sure not to go there?"

She patted his hand. "Right here with us," she smiled. "Right where we are now, just the other side of what everyone thinks is real. That's why it would be devastating if reality as we know it ever started to really unravel."

"I see." Mr. Perkins looked at Blast and wondered if pigs resented humans for their shameless mistreatment of them.

She pointed at Blast. "In alternate realities, magical moments seem to happen quite naturally. Pigs talk to horses, dogs play poker, and vultures eat in diners."

"Let's go." Blast, or Bogie depending on who saw him, walked up to the front door and stopped. He held out his brass key ring but there was no keyhole, just a thin slit where a key card would be inserted.

"I really think we should come back in the morning," Maga pleaded, but Blast had his own agenda. With athletic precision he drove his whole right side into the front door. Glass exploded and he stepped carefully through. "Let's go!" He turned to Maga. "Where?"

She pointed. "In my locker, down that hallway. Number 23."

An alarm sounded—a piercing, high-tech shriek loud enough to wake the neighborhood.

Blast clutched Mr. Perkins and Maga in his arms/trotters and practically flew to her locker.

As the police drew closer, their sirens grew louder.

Maga unlocked her locker and removed a colorful silk bag with a drawstring handle. It bulged with the wallets. She handed it to Blast. "Here! Now leave me alone."

But it was too late. Three policemen rushed through the shattered door and raced toward them.

"This is the police! All of you, raise your hands in the air and step apart from one another!" a tall, burly Sergeant shouted.

"You guys got this all wrong," Bogie said.

"Who are you?" asked a trim Captain in a well-pressed uniform.

"Marlow," Bogie said. "I'm a private eye from LA here on business."

"You broke into this building," the Captain said. "What kind of business is that?"

"Confidential," Bogie said.

"What do you mean 'confidential', you two-bit peeper?" the Captain roared. "Who do you think you're dealing with, some hick-town Gomer Pile police department?"

The Sergeant snatched the silk bag from Blast. "What's this?"

Mr. Perkins spoke up. "Officer, if you just allow me, I think I can explain everything."

The Sergeant whirled on Mr. Perkins. He waved his long flashlight. "You just wait your turn." Then he untied the cords and peered inside Maga's bag. He saw the leather wallets and promptly started sneezing. "I don't usually have an allergic reaction to leather. Whose bag is this?"

"It's mine," Maga said. "I keep the wallets here in my locker with my incense to sell at the Saturday craft shows."

"Yes," Mr. Perkins said. "I can attest to that."

Maga looked hard at Blast. "I sold them to his employer, who sent him here to retrieve them. He's terribly rude. Earlier today he barged in on Henry and me. I urged him to wait until tomorrow, when the Center was open." She waved her hand. "But as you can see, he's terribly impetuous with zilch for brains." She shifted on her feet. "I'm sure his employer will cover all damages." She smiled sweetly at the young Captain. "I'd appreciate it if you'd give them back to me."

But the Captain had other ideas. "We're taking you to the station, all three of you." He turned to the patrolman. "Secure the premises. He held onto Maga's bag. "Chief will want to see these and interrogate all of you."

Mr. Perkins and Maga were told to wait in one of the squad cars. They sat together in the back seat. Blast, alias Bogie, was jostled into the other cruiser with the Captain and the Sergeant.

"I hope you're all right, Henry." Maga said.

"Wolves," Mr. Perkins whispered. "They're all gray wolves in blue uniforms."

"It's because you're sensitive, Henry. You see deep into people's true nature." She smiled. "But if Zeke doesn't get those wallets back and mend the tear in the curtain that divides reality from everything else, then seeing people the way you do could become the new common cold."

"That would be different." He patted her paw. "How much time do you think there is before what you said happens?"

She shrugged. "Zeke's an astrologer. He knows how much time is left."

Mr. Perkins laughed. "Before the world goes mad."

"Don't say things like that Henry; you'll upset people."

"But oughtn't they to know that this might happen so they could prepare."

"This isn't really something to think about right now." She patted his hand with her paw.

The patrolman got in behind the wheel and the cruiser left the Center.

Minutes later they were at the station and seated in the small interrogation room. Almost immediately the Chief of Police strode in and confronted Mr. Perkins,

Maga, and Blast-a.k.a-Bogie sitting on folding chairs at a round metal table. He already knew the couple were residents with no criminal records. But something about this Marlow character rubbed him the wrong way.

He gave him a hard look. "What's the story here, Marlow? Why does a private peeper from LA kick down the door of our Senior Center?" He picked up Maga's bag. "Why the big rush?"

Blast glanced at his trotters that all but Mr. Perkins saw as Bogie's lean hands. "Like I said. My client's in a hurry."

The Chief's eyes narrowed. "So why you instead of Fed Ex?"

Marlow curled his rubbery lip. "Guess he likes the way I deliver."

Maga's heart sank as the Chief opened her drawstring bag and dumped the wallets onto the metal table. He looked at Marlow. "What's so special about these?"

"Couldn't tell ya," the words came out of the side of his mouth. "I only follow orders. I'm just a messenger boy."

"And your orders were to kick down that door?"

He shrugged. "Sometimes I don't know my own strength."

"Listen, you!" The Chief put his fists on the desk and leaned his considerable height in Blast/Bogie's direction. "I'm not fooling around!"

The Sergeant spread out the wallets. The Captain and two patrolmen came in.

The Chief looked at Mr. Perkins. "You seem like a model citizen: local homeowner for quite some time, never so much as parking ticket. So what's going on, Henry?"

Mr. Perkins looked at the Chief—to him a large gray white wolf with a white mane. "Most likely you won't believe a word I tell you."

"Most likely," the Chief smiled. "But tell me anyway."

Mr. Perkins pointed at Blast. "That man's a pig."

The Chief shook his head. "No need to call someone names, sir. I just want the facts."

"That *is* a fact. He *is* a pig." Mr. Perkins worked hard to control his voice. "Can't you see that? Isn't it obvious to you?"

The Chief sighed. He was getting nowhere. He wanted to be home in time for supper. "Did you do any *serious* drinking today, Henry?"

"I have no idea," Mr. Perkins replied. "I did enjoy a glass of sherry with my friend here," he looked at Maga and pointed at Bogie, "until he intruded."

The Chief rolled his eyes. "Why not start at the beginning?"

Mr. Perkins nodded. "I know exactly how you feel. This sort of thing can appear very confusing. All I can tell you is that those wallets are magical and that pig was sent here to get them back by someone in Arizona called Zeke."

The Chief tried to smile. "Magical? Magical how? Like something out of Harry Potter or more like a science fiction story with little green men who aren't there?"

"Exactly," Mr. Perkins nodded. "I'm glad you're starting to see this my way."

The Chief frowned. He realized that somehow he had lost the thread of the conversation. He turned to Maga. "And you said that he," pointing at Bogie, "broke into where you live and forced the two of you to drive to the Senior Center and, once inside, he took possession of that bag of wallets?"

"Yes," Maga nodded. "That's exactly what happened." She looked pleadingly at Mr. Perkins.

The Sergeant and the Captain opened the wallets and started looking inside.

"What's this?" the Captain exclaimed. A shower of hundred dollar bills spewed from the wallet. Henry and Maga looked at each other and shrugged,

"Where did these come from?" exclaimed the Sergeant. But before he could put the wallet down, a pile of hundreds cluttered up the table. For a moment Mr. Perkins thought he saw Benjamin Franklin laughing.

The Captain dropped the wallet and reached for another. He looked over at Bogie. "What's going on here?"

"It's real money!" the Sergeant said. The other officers began opening wallets also. The more wallets they opened the higher grew the tsunami of century notes cascading from the table onto the floor.

Once order had been restored in the interrogation room and the mountain of hundreds swept up, the Chief put his fists on his hips and glared. "Marlow, I'm holding you for destruction of property and breaking and entering a town building." He looked at the three large trash bags filled with hundreds. "And grand theft! You'll be booked in the morning. So if you've anything to say…" he nodded to the two patrolmen.

They braced Blast's shoulders. He slouched inside the folds of his trench coat and gave Maga a cockeyed wink. "Here's looking at you, kid." Then showing no resistance, his fedora sliding over his eyes, he sagged against the two patrolmen. As his full weight slumped into their arms their eyes widened.

The Chief's stomach growled. He had skipped lunch and it was telling him to go home to dinner. He followed the patrolmen into the corridor. "You'll need to get a hold of your lawyer." He watched them as they half dragged Blast to the elevator. The two patrolmen's faces reflected strain. By the time they jostled Blast from the elevator into the empty holding cell, they were breathing hard. Panting, they locked the cell door, returned to the small elevator and went back upstairs.

Blast/Bogie slid onto the small cot. His eyes were closed. Slowly the trench coat deflated until it covered him like a blanket. His mind began to drift. A short while later a thin brown ferret crawled out from under that blanket.

Quickly he made his way between the bars and into the corridor. He sniffed his way past several closed doors, and then surveyed the walls until he spotted a small opening. He climbed up to it and, hidden from sight, positioned himself to wait.

"The DA will take this one over," the Chief said as he came back into the interrogation room. He took his bottle of antacid pills from his pocket and swallowed two with the water from the bubbler. He wanted to go home.

He looked at Mr. Perkins and Maga. "You two check out as town residents," he told them. "I'm releasing you both on personal recognizance. But don't leave town until this wallet business is resolved. You can go home now."

They stood up. Maga nodded. "Thank you. It's been a very long day."

The Chief sighed. "They're all like that for a police officer." He turned to Mr. Perkins. "Let all this be a lesson to you." He looked him in the eye." If I were you, I'd hold off on that glass of sherry until closer to bedtime."

"I absolutely agree," Mr. Perkins stammered. "I'll try a lot harder."

"That's a good thing," the Chief said. "It's hard not to get involved with those carnival types around here."

"I'm not quite sure what you mean, but I'll certainly take what you said under consideration," Mr. Perkins said. Together they went out the door, and then, remembering Maga's car was back at the senior center, went back in and asked for a ride.

After asking a patrolman to give them a lift, the Chief said good night to the Captain and the Sergeant. "This is one case I wouldn't mind the State Police taking over. Be sure those wallets and trash bags are locked in the safe. Leave Marlow until morning. We'll deal with him then."

Back at the Senior Center, Henry and Maga climbed into her car. She sighed audibly, reached into her purse and took out a cigarette. "I hope you don't mind my smoking, Henry. I just need to unwind."

"I think we should go out to dinner," he said.

"Why not go back to my place so we can relax and pick up where we left off. I'll make a salad."

"You don't like restaurants?"

"That isn't it. I think, for your own well-being, avoiding restaurants just now might be smart." Mr. Perkins knew that pouty tone of voice. Helen had pouted her way through their marriage.

"Do you mind telling me why?"

She sighed "For you, any restaurant is likely to be filled with all sorts of strange creatures. I'd rather you didn't put yourself through such an ordeal."

"Oh, yes," he nodded. "Yes. I think I understand." What he understood was that trying to argue with this woman was senseless. But Helen had been that way. This one seemed to know how to come up with better reasons for her pronouncements.

Back at the cabin in the desert, daylight was fading. Zeke drank coffee and made careful notations on paper. Worried that time was running out, he turned the pages of his dog-eared astrological ephemeris as he waited for Blast to return with the wallets. He went to the cupboard and carefully removed the sacred iridescent stones he had found at the ancient ruins in the desert. He placed them on the long table in a pattern forming an ancient magical sigil.

Then, before sitting back down, he refilled his cup with the rich, dark coffee and took several swallows. Then he set it down, closed his eyes and concentrated on tasting it, inviting its flavor, its bouquet, and its aroma to captivate him. As his mind became completely focused on the coffee, he raised his hands, swept them over the sparkling stones, and was transported into the essence of Abracadabra Moonshine.

It was almost midnight in Arizona, nearly 3 a.m. back East. Zeke took some tobacco from a small pouch he kept for such purposes and carefully wrapped it in a spill of special, handmade paper. His mind settled itself into a steady focus on his breathing. His senses embraced the strong essence of the coffee until he was fully engaged in the present moment. His mind emptied and then filled with the velvety night around him and the sparkle of the far away stars.

Freed from the confines of his everyday mind, his spirit body found itself in a garden radiant with blossoms. Breathing in the fragrance of flowers, Zeke allowed himself to feel fully embraced within the magic of this place and the essence of Abracadabra Moonshine. He then placed tobacco upon a small stone altar and asked that any tears in the fabric of reality be mended and that all be returned to its normal state.

The effulgence of the garden was captivating. The full moon energy blazed through him. The sacred stones arranged on his long table glowed eerily in the dim cabin. He did not see them. His eyes were firmly shut. Chanting aloud he repeated nine times: "May all be made right and returned to the way it was before."

At that same moment back East, a brown ferret climbed from a crevice in the wall of the police station and scurried up a flight of stairs. It slinked behind the duty officer's desk and down a corridor to the chief's office. There it grew, and shape-shifted into Blast. He waved his trotters at the safe. It opened. He reached for Maga's cloth bag with the magical wallets, touched each trash bag, closed the safe door and vanished.

Blast reappeared in Zeke's cabin. He grunted and tossed Maga's bag onto the long table. Zeke snatched it up, took it outside and opened the cover to the incinerator. Adding a pinch of the tobacco, Zeke tossed in the wallets. He and Blast hurried back to the cabin.

The round face of the old railroad clock hanging above his bookcase read one minute to midnight. The sky exploded with lightning. A jolt struck the incinerator and it exploded.

The Chief's cell phone rang. Sliding out of bed so as not to wake his wife, he opened it. The night Sergeant seemed incoherent. "Gone!" He blurted. "Marlow escaped. He got out somehow. Cell's still locked."

The Chief sighed. "Start at the beginning."

"Routine check. Cell was locked and empty!"

The chief's stomach lurched. Whatever was going on was beyond his grasp.

"Tell me again!"

"Routine lock-up check at 3 a.m. The cell was empty, locked. Nothing tampered with. He just wasn't there."

"That's impossible!"

"Just the facts, Chief. There's nothing else to say."

"Get the Captain. I'll be right down."

He closed his phone and yawned. "Another day!" he sighed.

The chief's cruiser crept through town. As he passed the Senior Center he glanced at the door. It looked the same as always, nothing broken.

He pulled into the station's lot and hurried inside.

"All right, fill me in!"

The Captain yawned. "Just got here myself," he said. "Lock-up's empty. We dusted. Nothing. It's like Marlow was never even there."

"That's ridiculous! Of course he was in there! We put him there."

The Sergeant joined them. "Nothing outside. No vehicles detected from surveillance cameras. However he escaped, it wasn't in a vehicle."

"It's too early in the morning for these guessing games," the Chief growled. They followed him into his office. He punched in the complex code that opened the office safe. Maga's bag of magical wallets was gone. He pulled out the trash bags.

"At least they're still here," the Sergeant said.

The chief untied the first bag. Styrofoam cups and assorted trash fell out.

He untied the other. More trash.

"But we put those bills in there!" the Sergeant said.

"We saw each other do it," the Captain lamented.

"Of course you did," the Chief said. "Just like we put Marlow in the holding cell."

The men stared at each another.

"More to this than meets the eye!" the Chief said.

"Maybe we all go get some breakfast," the Captain said. "Coffee anyway. The diner's open all night."

At 8:30 Maga went into her guest room. "Henry? Are you awake yet?"

"I'm not sure," Mr. Perkins said. "Probably not. My mind seems to be spinning." He opened his eyes. He looked again. It was true! She wasn't a cat.

She raised the shade. Bright sunlight streamed into the room.

"It's you," he said. "You're the woman who gave me that infernal wallet." He smiled; his eyes widened. "And you're not a cat!"

"You mean you don't see me as a cat anymore? Oh, Henry, this must mean Zeke—"

"Made everything normal. And I can see you as you, as you are."

Her eyes widened. "You see me as I am!" She covered her face with her hands. "Don't look at me Henry. Turn your head away."

"Why?"

"I haven't put on my face yet. I'm not wearing my makeup."

"Helen hardly ever used the stuff. She thought it was too expensive." He reached for his glasses. "I'm just so glad to see you as you instead of as a cat."

"Thanks, Henry," she said with a smile. "I feel glad you do."

The Typewriter

Hank found the old, black, office-mode Underwood typewriter at a Saturday morning yard sale. Despite its antiquity, it was remarkably bright, in splendid working order. Even the ribbon appeared shiny and new.

He smiled at the woman having the sale and without quibbling paid her the five dollar sticker price.

"Yours from college?" he asked.

She smiled. "I hope I don't look that ancient. I had a PC back then. No, we found it here in the attic. The homeowner died suddenly and we bought the place from the bank."

Hank took his new treasure home and placed it on his work station next to his laptop. He put some typing paper beside it and went to the kitchen to make himself some lunch.

When he came back a sheet of the white paper was already in the roller. Had he put it there earlier? He wasn't sure.

Hank had managed to make it through some of Hemingway's short stories when he studied business at State before becoming a sales rep for Amalgamated Concrete. Something about this typewriter awoke a new-found impetus to try his hand at writing. He sat down in his desk chair.

He had no concept of plot or character development; he thought maybe that kind of stuff wasn't important and decided to let the stories flow on their own. He remembered a professor at State saying that Hemingway's stories wrote themselves.

He leaned back. In his mind's eye he saw an image of a terse, tough private eye who specialized in protecting rich high-society dames. Some of them were victims desperately seeking his help. Others were cold-blooded killers out to do him in. The detective's name was Johnny Hero.

Johnny used to run back punts for an NFL team before being sidelined by a knee injury. He didn't talk so good either. But there Hank ran out of gas and decided this writing business wasn't as easy as he had thought. He yawned, got up, went into the kitchen and got himself a beer. He took it out onto his deck, sat down and watched the leaves blow about the yard.

Back inside, he went to the typewriter and discovered four neatly typed pages awaiting him. The story read real good. His detective was strong, big, tough. He talked in small words. Hank liked small words. They were easy to understand.

The story was called *Lurid Lady*. "Thanks," he said wondering who was helping him write the story. More specifically, he couldn't help but wonder what exactly was going on.

The following morning the typewriter held a single sheet of paper with one typed word: whiskey. Hank drove to the package store and returned with a pint which he set down next to his typewriter. By supper that day the unopened bottle was empty.

Later that week Hank entered *Lurid Lady* in a short story contest. He won and he found himself three hundred dollars richer. This writing business seemed a lot easier and more profitable than hawking concrete for Amalgamated.

More stories featuring his big, tough private eye followed. Each had an unexpected ending, a twist that left the reader gasping. Someone equated his style to O'Henry's, others suggested Roald Dahl. Someone else asked if he had a graduate degree in Ambrose Bierce. Hank would just smile. He avoided discussing dead writers he knew nothing about.

The whiskey bottles emptied faster. Hank went to the package store daily. Though he didn't drink beyond his usual six pack a week he'd nonetheless wake up with a savage hangover. The stories continued to flow from the typewriter and he decided the whiskey was little enough price to pay for this new found literary output.

He was getting thinner. His trousers were looser, his shirts hung off his shoulders. He needed new clothes, several sizes smaller.

His co-workers at Amalgamated and his buddies from town gossiped that he looked older, more wizened. Was he drinking? Didn't he seem to have the shakes? Someone even had the audacity to suggest he go for counseling. "Concrete can do that to a man," a co-worker said.

Every story sold and soon he was earning close to a thousand per for this hard-edged, gutsy realism. His bank account bulged. He quit his job. His phone rang constantly from magazine editors who offered him contracts Hollywood agents called inviting him to fly out to Tinseltown to talk about scripts over lunch.

Meanwhile, Johnny Hero became more cynical and dark. His female clients lied through their teeth and he couldn't trust any of them. He lost his ability to differentiate between purity and mud.

His readers loved it and begged for more. A collected volume was to be published next spring. Hank became the current literary darling of the social media. Blogs praised his new found sense of gritty, urban realism. But Hank was becoming a recluse. He avoided practically everyone, especially women who'd try to flirt with him.

Things went on this way until one morning he stumbled into the kitchen and made some coffee. He carried his cup over to his work station. There was a piece of paper in the typewriter. *Perhaps this is the beginning of another story,* he thought. He pulled the paper from the roller. On it was a single sentence:

"No more, your turn now."

Acolyte   Stephen Halpert

Cover art drawn from *Acolyte*, a collage in the artist's
Miniature Gold Frame Series Number 3 (2012). See
Stephen's art: stephenhalpert.com.

About the Author

Stephen Halpert likes to explore and unearth historical relics and literary treasures. He discovered the archive of a literary magazine from the 1930s which he synthesized into *A Return to Pagany,* Beacon Press. He later uncovered glass negatives taken by an unknown Boston newspaper photographer, G. Frank Radway. From them was created a popular pictorial social history, *Brahmins and Bullyboys*, Houghton Mifflin. He also co-edited *Witness of the Berrigans,* Doubleday.

With his wife, Tasha, during the 1980s, he created Healing Arts Press. Together they published a number of esoteric and spiritual books, several cookbooks and two manuals of self healing. Since 1989 his weekly column, *American Scene* has appeared in *The Grafton News* and, more recently, on funnywrite.com.

Abracadabra Moonshine is also available as an audio-book and e-book.

To reach Stephen Halpert and find information on forthcoming titles visit: sandtpublishing.com.